SAFE AS
HOUSES

SAFE AS HOUSES

A MYSTERY BY

Susan Glickman

Cormorant Books

The publisher gratefully acknowledges the support of the Canada Council for the Arts and the
Ontario Arts Council for its publishing program. We acknowledge the financial support of the
Government of Canada through the Canada Book Fund (CBF) for our publishing activities, and
the Government of Ontario through the Ontario Media Development Corporation, an agency
of the Ontario Ministry of Culture, and the Ontario Book Publishing Tax Credit Program.

LIBRARY AND ARCHIVES CANADA CATALOGUING IN PUBLICATION

Glickman, Susan, 1953–, author
Safe as houses / Susan Glickman.

Issued in print and electronic formats.
ISBN 978-1-77086-436-8 (PBK.). — ISBN 978-1-77086-437-5
(html)

I. Title.

PS8563.L49S23 2015   C813'.54   C2014-907697-5
                                       C2014-907698-3

Cover photo and design: Angel Guerra/Archetype
Interior text design: Tannice Goddard, Soul Oasis Networking
Printer: Friesens

Printed and bound in Canada.

CORMORANT BOOKS INC.
10 ST. MARY STREET, SUITE 615, TORONTO, ONTARIO, M4Y 1P9
www.cormorantbooks.com

"Who can hope to be safe? Who sufficiently cautious? Guard himself as he may, every moment's an ambush."

— HORACE

THE FIRE was an animal let out of its cage. First it stood still, pondering a world without barriers. It put one tentative paw forward, then another. Then it leapt.

Thinking fast, he ran to the bathroom for a glass of water to throw on it. The flames retreated, hissing, for one hopeful moment; recovered and flared up higher than before. The room was getting hotter and hotter. No one else was home and he didn't know what to do.

He ran out of the house and into the untamed forest behind it. Usually he avoided the forest because Brian said it was full of bears and cougars and poisonous snakes, but today he was less afraid of wild animals than he was of the creature prowling in the house.

He had just reached the shelter of the trees when he heard voices, one of them his foster mother's, calling his name, but he was too afraid to respond. Although he'd been punished often — usually when he had no clue what he had done wrong and sometimes when he'd done nothing at all — this time he knew exactly what he had done. It was a crime. And if his punishment fit his crime, he doubted he would survive it.

The branches scratched his arms till they bled and his right hand throbbed terribly where the sizzling glue had stuck to it, but he ignored the pain. It wasn't the first time he'd been burned; little round scars up and down his arms attested to that. He knew that eventually the burn would stop hurting: a blister would fill with water and the blister would burst, revealing new pink skin underneath. If only he could start over the same way.

He scrunched down in the dirt and tried to make himself even smaller and more invisible than he usually was. Maybe Brian was right, and there were poisonous snakes out here in the forest. He hoped Brian was right; he hoped one would bite him. Then it would be over, once and for all. He would never have to look at angry faces or hear angry voices again.

Liz Ryerson woke up early Sunday morning. Too early, because Sunday was the only day she didn't open her bookstore, the only day she could sleep in. At first she didn't know what had roused her, but soon enough she recognized the familiar sounds of laughter and music coming from upstairs.

"Damn it, Adam," she said, startling Jasper out of his twitchy slumber.

The dog lifted his head from where he sprawled across the foot of the bed and assessed the situation. She was talking to herself, as usual. Satisfied that his services were not required, Jasper flopped back down immediately. But there was no way Liz could relax, hearing her ex-husband and his latest girlfriend doing things she preferred not to imagine right above her head. In the last few months Adam had given up trying to be discreet. Liz wasn't sure whether it was because he was really in love this time or because he no longer cared how she felt; whatever the reason, his behaviour was getting on her nerves.

Having Adam around had made sense when they'd split up five years ago. They owned the building jointly and since her bookstore was at street level and his photography studio on the third floor, neither of them wanted to go through the agony of moving. Besides, if Adam moved back into his studio — the same studio he had been living in when he and Liz first met — Joshua and Samantha would continue to have two resident parents. Despite the incredulity of their friends and relations, the arrangement had worked remarkably well, mainly because the kids loved it but also because, despite everything, she and Adam had remained friends.

Still, it would have taken a lot more patience than Liz possessed to flip her pillow over to the cool side and turn the other cheek. She sighed, then wriggled her legs out from under the dog, swung them over the side of the bed, and shuffled off to make coffee. Jasper lapped at his water bowl to keep her company, then wolfed down two cups of organic human-grade kibble as though he hadn't eaten in days.

"Give me a minute to get dressed and then I'll take you outside," Liz said, putting down her empty mug.

She walked back to the bedroom to pull on jeans and a turtleneck, adding a fleece sweater to combat the autumn chill. For once it wasn't raining, but it would still be prudent to wear rubber boots. Fully equipped, she dropped her house key in her pocket, snapped Jasper's leash onto the ring on his collar, and the two of them ran happily down the stairs to St. Clair. The street was wrapped in its Sunday vestments, the quiet broken only by church bells and the rumble of passing streetcars.

As part of an ongoing campaign to get more adolescent help around the house, Liz had briefly considered asking her kids to take the dog out, but Jasper's morning walk couldn't wait until they stumbled out of hibernation sometime around noon. And to be honest, unlike schlepping the garbage cans out to the street or doing the laundry, walking Jasper was not a chore she resented. She actually looked forward to it. Their walks were like parentheses, enclosing the daylight hours; walking, her thoughts moved according to their natural rhythm and she didn't have to explain herself to anybody. She might come upon a forgotten memory the way she discovered a yellow magnolia tree lit with a thousand aromatic candles, or a cardboard box inscribed "Free to Good Home" stuffed full of action figures, or a love poem by Federico Garcia Lorca blowing down the street: "*La mar no tiene naranjas, / ni Sevilla tiene amor.*" Walking, she could forget that she had become a wide-hipped, middle-aged divorcée and be the person she still felt herself to be inside.

Sometimes she thought the fact that she'd never been an "Elizabeth" to anyone but her mother and the occasional school-teacher must announce to the world — and to those worldlier than she — that she'd never grown up. After all, she'd never bought a lottery ticket or got stinking drunk or taken a package vacation; she'd never had a one-night stand or a professional manicure. She'd only worn really high heels once, at her room-mate Melanie's wedding, when she'd dyed a pair of stilettos to match the green silk bridesmaid's dress that had been intended to set off her blond hair but instead cast a sickly patina over her habitual pallor. Because she couldn't balance properly in them, the effect had been closer to wilted celery than to English rose.

That was the night that she fell in love with Adam, Melanie's cousin.

She'd been sneaking glances at him all evening, although she couldn't have said why. Something about the way his saturnine face became incandescent when he smiled? Or maybe it was the red high-top sneakers winking at her below his conservative dark suit? At any rate, once she had kicked off her own lethal shoes she limped over to the bar, where he was drinking beer straight from the bottle while watching a limbo competition with deadpan attentiveness. She hadn't realized that her interest in him was so obvious until he crossed his beautiful hazel eyes and peered up into her myopic blue ones, intoning solemnly, in his best (stagy, unconvincing, but to her ears utterly charming) imitation of an English accent, "Our vegetable love should grow/ Vaster than empires, and more slow."

"PARDON?" ASKED AN ELDERLY gent burdened by shopping bags, who had been negotiating the crosswalk at Christie Street and arrived at the curb just in time to hear her murmuring: "But at my back I always hear/ Time's wingèd chariot drawing near." Jasper trotted up to the man, tail wagging furiously. Groceries always made him happy. Happy and hopeful.

"I'm so sorry. I was just thinking out loud," Liz replied, embarrassed. "Get down, Jasper!"

"Well, I'm glad to know I'm not the only one who does that," the man laughed. "Talking to myself, I mean, not jumping up on strangers."

"I hope he didn't get you dirty."

"No, I'm fine. What kind of dog is he, some sort of retriever?"

"Probably part Labrador and part border collie. We got him from the Humane Society, so I don't really know. Do you like dogs?"

"Better than I like most people. Although I have to say this seems to be a friendly neighbourhood."

"Did you just move here?"

"Yes, a couple of months ago."

"Welcome to Hillcrest Village. My name is Liz Ryerson. I run the bookstore over on St. Clair."

"Maxime Bertrand." He put his bags down to shake her hand. "I don't remember seeing a bookstore on St. Clair. What's it called?"

"Outside of a Dog. I'm not surprised you didn't realize it was a bookstore; people often don't until they look in the window. And even then plenty of them come in asking for pet food or goldfish."

"Why did you pick such an odd name? If you don't mind my asking."

Bored by the conversation, Jasper butted his head up against the man's thigh, demanding to be scratched behind the ears.

"It's from my favourite quotation: 'Outside of a dog, a book is a man's best friend. Inside of a dog, it's too dark to read.' Marx, of course. Not Karl. Groucho."

"Well, I look forward to visiting you both there," Maxime

Bertrand said, giving Jasper's silky ears a final tug before picking up his grocery bags and continuing on his way.

"OKAY. NO MORE TALKING. Just walking," Liz said to Jasper as she turned into the private enclave at Wychwood Park.

They walked the loop around the pond daily, allowing Liz to observe the minutiae of the changing seasons and providing Jasper with frequent opportunities to harass the resident ducks. For their part, the mallards were unimpressed. Presumably he wasn't the only dog to bark at them and, on a leash on the other side of a fence, he was clearly less dangerous than the foxes and raccoons that occasionally invaded their space. Whatever the reason for their indifference, the ducks' refusal to be startled drove Jasper to frantic fits of barking followed by a great show of digging under the fence. When Liz judged he had satisfied enough of his inner Great and Fearless Hunter of Annoying Feathered Creatures, she would rein him in and resume their walk past the area's elegant houses, trying to look like she wasn't the one with the out-of-control pet whose yapping had disturbed their moneyed tranquility.

Her friends had said she was crazy to get a dog when she was starting up a new business, but it had worked out well. Sometimes people who weren't particularly bookish were lured inside by the eccentric name of the store; others were enticed by the shaggy affability of Jasper himself. A remarkable number of ordinary-looking folk seemed unable to walk past any dog without greeting it, even if that dog lay snoring in the sun pouring through a dusty plate glass window, surrounded by piles of second-hand books. A good many of those who came into the shop to pat Jasper left quickly, their mission accomplished, but plenty of others made unanticipated purchases. Apart from his usefulness in attracting customers, Jasper offered Liz companionship on days when things were slow, constant if somewhat sloppy affection, and a good excuse to roam her neighbourhood regardless of the weather.

She had always loved walking. When she was a kid in Prince Edward Island, her dad used to take Liz and her brother Michael for long hikes every Sunday so their mother could give the house "a proper cleaning." Their mother liked to do things by herself; at least on Sundays her preference for solitude and their father's desire to be outside were complementary. Mr. Ryerson was a serious "twitcher" back before the British passion for bird-watching had caught on in North America, so he was glad of any excuse to take off with a pair of binoculars and Peterson's *Guide to the Birds of North America*, even if it meant he had to bring the children with him.

Liz's father was as quiet as her mother but his silence was more companionable. Sometimes she thought he had taken up bird-watching as an excuse to avoid conversation, but in her more charitable moments she understood that it was the perfect expression of who he really was: a Yorkshire lad happiest rambling on the moors. It was actually this love of the countryside that drove him away from home, unable to bear the prospect of a life down the mines with his father and brothers and assorted bitter, hard-drinking cousins. Eventually he found work with Wills Tobacco in Bristol; it was an environment more dangerous than the one he'd fled, as he began to smoke cigarettes there and remained an unrepentant pack-a-day man for the rest of his short life.

It was also at Wills that he met her mother, the prettiest girl at the works. And it was her mother's desire for a house like the one in the photographs her cousin Betty sent from Vancouver — so new and big and clean, centrally heated, with its own attached garage — that had brought the family to Canada. Liz's father landed a job with the burgeoning tobacco industry on the island and her mother acquired the house she had dreamed of, and with it an obsession with cleanliness that verged on the pathological. Liz and Michael, worried about moving so far away from family and friends, had been promised a dog when they got to their new home. But the thought of a dog tracking mud on her gleaming parquet, a dog shedding all over her precious broadloom, a dog digging up her flowerbeds, was too much for their mother to bear. So that was that. Still, Liz often thought about how much her father and Jasper would have loved each other and imagined them out walking together, her father whistling, the air rushing effortlessly through healthy lungs.

JASPER'S EXCITED PANTING HAD ratcheted up to a threatening growl and finally to outright barking, reminding her that they were approaching the pond. A flotilla of ducks immediately swam over, their small but resourceful brains equating visitors with food. She never bothered to bring any treats for the birds, assuming that the folk in the big houses all around took good care of them. These plump specimens were far from undernourished. How impossibly glossy the males' heads were, rippling from purple to jade as the light hit their feathers. She'd once had a moiré skirt that shimmered like the northern lights in exactly that way.

Liz dragged the dog up the road away from the ducks but, to her surprise, he didn't stop barking as he usually did.

"Shut up, Jasper," she said in exasperation.

Ignoring her, he pulled harder on his leash.

"What is it, boy?"

His barking grew more frantic and she found herself almost running to lighten the tension on his collar. She followed him around the edge of the chicken-wire fence, ignoring the signs reading DANGER! DEEP WATER AND QUICKSAND. She followed him down towards the marshy area between the tennis courts and the pond where, one spring, she had seen a Baltimore oriole blooming up from the weeds, as distinct as a scarlet flower. The oriole had sung his heart out for a good fifteen minutes while all around him fluttered those little yellow finches her father never had any trouble identifying but all looked the same to her. There were wonderful birds here, including red-tailed hawks and great blue herons. And other creatures, too; the whole place was a miniature nature reserve.

Slipping on fallen leaves the consistency of boiled cabbage, it suddenly occurred to Liz that Jasper was most likely on the trail of a gopher or a rabbit or worse, a skunk, and since he'd already been sprayed once by the latter with noxious effects that had permeated all their lives for the better part of a month, she would be foolish to let him dictate where they went today.

"Jasper! Sit and stay."

She pulled hard on the leash, making the dog gasp for air.

Lowering his haunches reluctantly to the muddy ground, he turned his head, fixing his eyes upon her, willing her to understand the intensity of his gaze. An uncanny noise vibrated low in his throat. It didn't sound like he was complaining about being choked. It didn't sound like an invitation to play. It didn't sound like he wanted to track any of the creatures of the boreal forest. In fact, it sounded like nothing she'd ever heard from her dog before.

Just beyond Jasper was a gate, kept firmly locked by the residents' association to prevent accidental drownings, and in front of the gate lay a briefcase. Perhaps someone had thrown it over the fence as a prank? Odd things did show up here from time to time, most notoriously a big metal safe that had been stolen from a fancy condominium many miles away: a safe that lay buried deep under snow until the spring thaw. By the time it was discovered it was quite empty, although some sodden papers scattered about had helped the park manager determine its owner. When Liz was told this story she naturally assumed, as the park manager had done himself, that the safe contained gold bullion or heirloom jewels or some other priceless treasure. But in fact, the only thing its owner regretted losing was the manuscript of an unfinished novel, the secret labour of many years.

Remembering this story made Liz decide to fetch the briefcase; you never knew what could be valuable to another person, and today it was her turn to be a good citizen.

"Stay," she repeated firmly to Jasper, as she picked her way down the slippery slope.

She was just opening the briefcase — fine leather, in good shape, it couldn't have been out there very long — to see who it belonged to when something else caught her eye: an unexpected sparkle in the churned-up mud. As she walked towards it, the sparkle solidified into a silver watch glinting out from under a pile of autumn leaves. It hadn't been visible from the distance, but the closer she got to it the better she understood what had upset her dog: a smell that even her inadequate human nose could identify. A smell that told her that the watch was still attached to a body and that the body it was attached to was most assuredly dead.

"WHAT MADE YOU COME down here?"

The homicide detective waited politely for her answer, a crumpled yellow notepad on his knee, his pen hovering above it like a glittering blue dragonfly. He was left-handed. Left-handed people tend to be creative, Liz thought to herself, irrelevantly. Because their right brain was dominant, presumably. Also, if you tried to make a left-handed child switch to using his right he would develop a stutter, because the motor and verbal functions would be forced to trade hemispheres. She couldn't remember where she'd read this but it was the kind of trivia she tended to remember at odd moments.

Especially when she was stressed.

"I was walking my dog and he just took off," she replied, trying to stay on track.

Jasper's warm body was pressed tightly against her right leg, his head resting on her knee where her hand stroked him compulsively; he could always tell when she was upset and needed the comfort of his presence.

"Did you see anybody running away from the area?"

"No. Jasper must have been following the smell. Once I found a dead cat in my neighbour's bushes; that really stank but this smells even worse. How come nobody noticed?"

In spite of her resolve to remain calm, Liz found herself crying again. They were sitting on a bench overlooking the tennis court while some forensic officers, including a photographer and a woman with a case full of instruments, were doing things she preferred not to see a hundred metres or so away. The scene-of-the-crime team all wore white latex gloves, reminding her bizarrely of her mother going to church, impeccably groomed long after other people had begun to dress more casually, the minister himself strumming a guitar and reading sentimental poems about universal brotherhood.

Liz sipped at the mug of strong sweet tea she had been given, presumably by the lady from whose house she had called 911. She was blond, sixtyish, well groomed; that's all Liz could remember, except the Arts and Crafts foyer with oak panelling and red and gold vintage wallpaper. She doubted she would recognize the woman again though she would have to give the mug back at some point. But everything that happened today seemed hazy and unreal; her blood was still drumming in her head so insistently that she thought she might faint. Even this man talking gently to her kept fading in and out of her awareness as though she was recovering from surgery.

Maybe she made that unlikely connection because he had the same reassuring manner as the obstetrician who delivered her twins by Caesarean section. "Take your time, Ms. Ryerson," he was saying now, as though that would solve anything. Next she expected him to say "just relax" or "keep breathing."

"I don't need more time, officer; I just don't have anything else to say. What do you need to know besides the fact that there's a body down there? I can't believe it. Even when they drained the pond a few years ago they found nothing but turtles, carp, and duckweed. This is such a peaceful place."

"Do you often walk your dog here?"

"Most days."

"Have you noticed anything suspicious recently?"

"What do you mean?" Liz asked, bewildered.

"Have you noticed any unusual activity, or people who don't belong?"

"There are so many strangers around here, it would be hard to tell."

"What do you mean by 'strangers'?" Now it was the detective's turn to look confused.

"I just mean people walking their dogs or taking a shortcut to Davenport, or delivery vans dropping off stuff. Besides which, the whole neighbourhood is under construction: first they fixed the gas mains and then they repaved the roads and then some genius decided they needed to replace the sewers so everything got dug up all over again."

"I understand," the detective said.

He had a very soothing voice: the kind of voice Liz thought of as cognac and associated with radio hosts. It had a slight, almost undetectable Caribbean lilt and suited the burnished tone of his skin. What had led a handsome, well-spoken fellow like him into something as grisly as homicide investigation? Would it be rude to ask?

Liz wondered frequently why people ended up doing the jobs they did, maybe because she'd never really planned a career for herself. Everything she'd done she'd fallen into, impulsively, because it seemed like a good idea at the time. Two years as a kindergarten assistant had disabused her of the notion that she had the right temperament to instruct midgets with runny noses, shrieking voices, and the attention span of crickets. A friend's suggestion that anyone who loved books as much as she did should become a librarian — coupled with a fervent need to leave home — brought her to the Faculty of Information Science in Toronto. After graduating, she'd worked as an archivist for little more than a year before finding herself uncomfortably pregnant with twins and giving up her job, returning part-time three years later. The bookstore had only come about because the man who ran the antique store previously occupying the retail space retired, and offered her twenty boxes of old books for free as a going-away present.

The detective scribbled away for a couple of minutes before flipping the page of his notepad and turning his attention to her again.

"Okay, Ms. Ryerson, let's move on. What about the place where you found the body? When was the last time you were down there?"

"Actually, this was the first time. I followed Jasper there because he was acting so weird."

"So, the body could have been lying in that spot for several days without your seeing it?"

"I suppose so." She gave a little shiver and bent down to bury her face in Jasper's fur.

"Well, it is pretty secluded," the detective conceded. "That's probably why he picked it."

"He?" she asked, finally meeting his eyes, curiosity over-coming distress. "Do you mean the dead man or somebody else? Are you suggesting this was murder?"

"It's too soon to say. We'll have to wait for the autopsy."

"No, we won't," said an older, fatter policeman, lumbering up the hill in time to overhear the last part of their conversation. The original officer to arrive on the scene, he seemed beside himself with ill-suppressed excitement. The local beat included the occasional burglary and auto theft, but not homicide.

"Blunt force trauma. The victim's skull was bashed in by a heavy object," he continued, practically chortling with glee.

"How do you know somebody hit him?" Liz objected. The possibility of violence in this idyllic setting was unthinkable. "Isn't it more likely he just fell down and smashed his head on a rock? It's pretty slippery with all these rotting leaves everywhere."

"Yeah, you're probably right," the fat policeman said, realizing from the look on the detective's face that he was going to get into trouble for giving away facts about the investigation prema-turely. "I nearly took a tumble myself."

"And he was wearing shoes with smooth soles just like you are," Liz added.

"How did you see his shoes? I thought the guy was buried in leaves."

"One foot was sticking out a bit at the bottom. Don't worry; I didn't touch anything."

"Unfortunately, you did," the detective who had been interviewing her broke in. "When you picked up that briefcase you contaminated crucial evidence, Ms. Ryerson. I know you didn't intend to, but your fingerprints are probably all over the damn thing."

"I'm very sorry, officer. I picked it up before I found the body."

"And?"

"And what?"

"And what did you find out from looking through the brief-case?" the detective continued, as though talking to a child.

"Well," Liz said, hoping that the information she was about to reveal would redeem his opinion of her, "the briefcase belonged to a real estate agent named James Scott and I'm pretty sure that's who the dead man is. He's the right height and build, from what I could see."

"You actually know the victim?" asked the other policeman, avidly. "Great! So what can you tell us about him?"

"Constable MacDonald, would you kindly shut up? This is a murder investigation, not a game show," snapped the detective.

"Mr. Scott deals with" — she swallowed, feeling sick as she remembered shaking the dead man's hand and saying she'd get back to him soon — "I mean, he *dealt* with a lot of property in this neighbourhood. In fact, he gave me an appraisal a couple of months ago, when I wanted to know what my own building was worth. He seemed honest. Hard-working."

"In other words, you can't tell us about the deceased that we couldn't find out by going through the briefcase ourselves," the detective said bluntly, getting up. Jasper immediately stood up too, relieved that this interminable conversation was over and they could resume their walk.

"I guess not," Liz said, lurching unsteadily to her own feet. She thought she might throw up. "Is there anything more I can do to help?"

"Here's my card, in case you remember anything else about what you saw or heard today. Call any time," he replied, putting a hand out to steady her, feeling remorseful for his fit of bad temper. He recognized the horrified expression on her face and knew it meant she would not find it easy to leave this experience behind. Not that anyone could — or should — walk away from violent death untouched; he'd never been able to do so himself.

"Of course, Detective Sergeant Wentworth," said Liz, reading his name off the card.

"You may not realize it, but you're in shock right now. Constable MacDonald will drive you wherever you like."

"Thanks, but I really want to walk home. Walking will make me feel better."

"Will anyone be there?"

"No, my kids are both at school."

"Well, get someone else to come over, okay?" Wentworth said in a kinder voice than he had used for a while. "You shouldn't be alone right now."

Liz craned her neck around, trying to remember which house she had called the police from so that she could return the mug still clutched in her hand. To her surprise, a sizable crowd had gathered, though they were held at a safe distance by MacDonald's partner, an Asian woman with a shining black bob. When they'd first driven up, Liz had been far too upset to notice what an incongruous couple they made, but now she found herself wondering whether the woman, who looked so poised and efficient, was frustrated by her partner's ineptitude. From the hang-dog expression on his face, she could see that MacDonald was being reprimanded by Wentworth, whose own partner from the Homicide division, an absurdly young-looking man he'd introduced as Detective Carson, was busy containing the area with yellow crime scene tape. Though she'd had a general awareness of activity at the periphery of her vision, she was amazed that she hadn't heard all those people behind her, buzzing like a swarm of giant insects. Or maybe she had heard them but their presence had just blended into the larger strangeness of the day.

Suddenly, someone blond stepped out of the throng and started waving at her. Assuming that this had to be the lady she was looking for, Liz said goodbye to the policemen and walked over to her, holding out the empty mug.

"Thanks for the tea," she said. "I really needed it."

"You're welcome. Did you find out what happened?"

As Liz wondered what she ought to say, more and more people crowded around, clamouring with questions and observations.

"Is it true that there's a body down there?"

"How did you find it?"

"I know her, she's the bookstore lady!"

"What's going on, Liz?" one of her regulars asked.

Liz suddenly realized that it would be impossible to keep her involvement in this gruesome event secret; she'd already been seen by people who recognized her. But if she tried to answer their questions she'd be stuck here for ages. So she replied evasively.

"Yes, there's a body down there below the tennis courts; my dog found it. But you'll have to ask the police if you want to know anything more."

And as the crowd surged forward to do just that, she and Jasper sprinted off, the dog gripping his leash in his mouth to remind her that he knew the way home and that they should go there immediately. But there was no way she could open the shop today. The news that its proprietor had stumbled upon a body in Wychwood Park would fly around the neighbourhood so fast that hordes of people would drop by in pursuit of gory details. The last thing Liz wanted right now was conversation — at least not that kind of conversation, gossipy and speculative. What she really wanted was to be alone; to think about what she'd seen. If she could think, that was; her head still felt so foggy.

Clearly, she needed more tea. Although she had lived in Canada since the age of six, the traditional English panacea still worked its magic on her. Adam had often joked that if they were ever in a car crash, the first thing Liz would ask would not be "Are you all right?" but "Fancy a cup of tea?" This wasn't exactly a car crash, and she wasn't the one who was hurt, but she found herself inadvertently smiling when she realized how closely she conformed to his expectations. And then she burst into tears.

DESPITE THE sirens and the voices screaming, despite the roots and rocks digging into him, despite the pain in his hand and the way his stomach churned with guilt and fear, he managed to fall asleep, his face pillowed on his arms, his fists full of dirt. He stayed hidden until morning when the provincial police arrived with a tracker dog. Its triumphant barking woke him up and although he tried to shoo it away and then burrow deeper under the boughs of an enormous pine tree, he was dragged from his refuge into daylight in front of a crowd of worried faces, most of them belonging to strangers.

At first no one was mad at him; they were just relieved that he hadn't died in the blaze. He drank two cups of sweet milky tea and let a lady from a farm down the road wash his face and wrap him in a blanket because he was dirty, wet with dew, and shivering with cold. She called him "honey" and "poor lamb" and told him everything would be all right. The lady had a wandering eye that made it hard to concentrate on what she was saying, but she smelled like warm bread and her hand holding his was as small and dainty as a child's.

Maybe he could go home with this new lady. Maybe nobody would discover what he had done and people would still want him to be their boy. He tried to lie, saying he didn't know what they were talking about, the fire wasn't his fault, he just ran away and hid because he was scared. But his burned hand and the glue on his clothes betrayed him. It didn't take long until the firemen figured everything out — how he'd held a lit match to the "Flying Fortress" model airplane Brian had been building; how the fire had spread quickly because there was glue spilled in Brian's messy room; how he'd been unable to put it out. So the farm lady gave him a last mournful look from her one good eye and went home. She let him keep the blanket.

BRIAN WAS hysterical. He tried to punch him in the face. He called him a son of a bitch and a murderer and a yellow-bellied coward. That didn't surprise him. Brian was a bully and everybody but his mother knew it. And everybody but his mother hated him.

Or maybe she had suspected something and that's why she had decided to take in a foster kid. Maybe she was disappointed her own child was so mean and was hoping to get a better one. Or maybe she just wanted to teach Brian how to be nice by setting a good example. Whatever her motivation — and unlike some of the other families he'd lived with, she didn't seem to be driven by the small sum of money social services paid for his care — it didn't work. As soon as her back was turned, Brian tormented him. The first night he came to their house he was so scared he peed the bed. Brian told everybody at school that his foster brother was a stinky little bedwetter, so nobody wanted to sit next to him or talk to him. When he eventually got up the courage to ask Brian to please stop calling him names, Brian just laughed. Later that same night Brian snuck into his room, pulled down his pyjama bottoms, and peed on the bed with him in it. Another time, when he had done well on a history test, Brian told the teacher he had cheated. The teacher, who had liked him and thought he was smart, never trusted him again.

He was afraid of Brian, as he had always been afraid of bullies. But more than that, he hated him. Still, he never meant to hurt Brian's mother. She was gentle and soft and a good cook, and she always treated him kindly. So when he finally understood what the people around him were saying — that she'd been killed running back into the burning house to try to save him — the world went dark in front of his eyes. He passed out.

After he came to, a policeman asked him if he wanted to explain his actions. All he could do was shake his head and cry. It was true that right before he set the fire Brian had ripped up the only picture he possessed of his own mother, calling her a drunken whore. But he knew that the police wouldn't think that was a good enough reason to burn down someone's house,

so all he said was that it was an accident, which was the truth —
he'd just wanted to ruin one of Brian's model airplanes to pay
him back for destroying the photograph.

Nobody believed him. He didn't expect them to. He had been
in the child-welfare system for too many years already.

HE WAS taken to the jail in town, the jail that only had one
cell. Even though he was barely thirteen and looked much
younger than his age, they locked him in with another prisoner,
a man who smelled of booze the way his own mother smelled
of booze in the bad times: the times he got taken away and
sent to foster care. Because of that smell he wasn't completely
surprised when the man pinned him down on his bunk and
did horrible things to him in the night. He knew what the man
did was wrong, but since he felt he deserved to be punished
he closed his eyes and gritted his teeth and told himself he
was bad, he had always been bad, and that's why bad things
happened to him.

When the man was finished, he closed huge hands around
his neck until he couldn't breathe and said he would kill him
if he ever told a soul what had happened. When the guard
checked on them in the morning and found him crying in
one corner of the cell, he said nothing. The guard looked sus-
piciously at the other prisoner, snoring on his cot, scratching
his crotch in his sleep, then shrugged and changed the bandage
on the boy's hand, assuming that was what was bothering him.

"Does it burn?" asked the guard.

"Yes," the boy answered. "Like hell."

3

"WOW; A REAL LIVE murder mystery to solve! The first thing we have to do is find out who the guy pissed off so badly that he whacked him," Josh declared at once.

"Josh, this isn't a joke," Liz protested. "A nice man, a man I actually knew, was just murdered."

"People are murdered every day, Mum."

"Not in my backyard they're not."

"Well, maybe we've been lucky so far," Sam added.

"I'd hate to think that it's just a matter of luck. Because then none of us is safe," Liz sighed.

"None of us is," Josh insisted. "You can try to shut out all the bad news and live in a bubble or you can go out and take what comes."

"Since when are you such a tough guy, Mr. Addicted-to-Cute-Animal-Videos? And are you implying that I live in a bubble?"

"You have to admit that you're kind of isolated from reality, Mum. All you do is read books, drink tea, and go for walks."

"I don't like the way this conversation is going," Liz said. "Something horrible happens and instead of saying 'Poor Mummy' and trying to make me feel better, you guys are attacking me."

"Poor Mummy," said Sam obediently. "It must have been awful."

"Yes, it was. And although the way your brother expressed himself was inappropriate, I agree with his sentiment. I hope the police figure out quickly who did this, and why, so that things can get back to normal."

Remembering this conversation made Liz wonder what kind of progress the police were making with the case. It had been a week since she'd stumbled on the body and, except for brief articles the first couple of days, there had been no news about the investigation.

Searching "James Scott" was interesting, but not particularly helpful. For one thing, there were a ton of guys with that name online. One of them was an Australian jazz trumpeter who liked to wear funny hats and another was a sushi chef in Glasgow; a third, who preferred to be called "Jim," had placed respectably in the Ironman triathlon and yet another, a stout and jolly epicure, was celebrating his fortieth wedding anniversary to his high-school sweetheart by taking his five children and fourteen grandchildren to the south of France for two weeks.

Where do you find a man like that? Liz wondered. There were a couple of others who were also real estate agents, though not here in Toronto. And those entries related to local real estate were mostly listings of property for sale or notices about industry events James Scott had attended or awards he had won rather than intimate glimpses of the fellow himself.

Liz had told the story of her gruesome discovery several times, not just to the police and her children but also to her shop assistant Georgia, whose habitual composure had been shaken when she understood how close, geographically, the murder was to her place of employment. But retelling the story was compulsive, not cathartic; it didn't make Liz feel any better. Nor did it help her remember an overlooked clue as she had hoped it might. There hadn't been much to see, except for the silver watch glinting from a pile of muddy leaves and one foot sticking out, as though trying to escape. She'd been so shocked by the sight of that foot, its white ankle vulnerably bare above a black sock, she'd sprinted straight to the nearest house and telephone without scrutinizing the scene further, throwing down the briefcase as though it were on fire.

A surprising number of people had already heard about the murder from other sources, but that didn't mean they were content to receive their gossip second-hand. Her phone had rung off the hook all week as the news that "the bookstore lady found a dead body" travelled throughout Hillcrest Village. She tried to keep these phone calls short — which wasn't hard because although a few people recognized James Scott's name, nobody knew much about him except that he was young and successful. And even though Liz herself had found the man both pleasant and professional, she realized in retrospect that she knew virtually nothing about him. It didn't help that when they'd met, she had been so overwhelmed by anxiety at the prospect of maybe, someday, having to sell her beloved building that she hadn't been as attentive as usual.

Many of the people eager to talk to Liz were quick to suggest that the murdered man's business was somehow implicated in his death. They assumed he must have been involved in some kind of shady deal — taking kickbacks from mortgage lenders or paying off home inspectors or some such thing. Almost everyone had horror stories about Toronto real estate: the house that had no heating system and was sold with unattached radiators leaning up against the walls; the house with a mouldy basement newly carpeted over; the couple who overpaid hugely for a run-down dump because their agent told them they were bidding against three other couples when they weren't. Even at her favourite patisserie, the Gâteau Basque, an elegant white-haired lady enjoying a midmorning café au lait and croissant had insisted with surprising acerbity that "he deserved it, because those greedy real estate people are ruining the neighbourhood."

"Come on, you can't blame the agents," objected one of the youths who ran between the kitchen and the cash register, arranging an exquisite tart in a nest of tissue paper before securing the pastry box with a swirl of gilt ribbons. "They didn't create the housing boom, they're just profiting from it."

"They certainly are profiting," said the lady's escort, whose own white hair was as carefully groomed as hers and whose moustache suggested he ought to be wearing a monocle rather than the horn-rimmed reading glasses perched on the end of his nose.

Peering over them at the other patrons of the patisserie, he continued, "Meanwhile, nobody knows what their property is really worth."

"It's a shame that young families can't afford to live around here anymore," Liz agreed.

"Well, who has half a million dollars for a starter home?" asked a tiny girl in yoga gear. She looked about twelve years old except for the diamond sparkling on the ring finger of her left hand and the fact that she was drinking a double espresso. "My boyfriend and I are living in a crummy bachelor apartment so that we can save enough for a down payment on a house. It really sucks."

"My real estate agent was an absolute doll," added a tired-looking young mother wiping chocolatey drool off the chin of her little boy. The child kept pushing her hands away and drumming his feet against his stroller in protest. "She bought us a lilac tree as a housewarming present and planted it herself," the woman continued, her child screaming so loudly the cook peered out of the kitchen to see what was going on.

"Get me her business card and I'll pin it up on the bulletin board in my bookstore," said Liz. "People are always asking if I know a decent agent."

"Sure," said the mother, who was now struggling to get the boy's hat on despite his arching neck and flailing arms.

A plate smashed to the ground and broke and then her diaper bag went flying. Liz helped her pick up the pieces of china and the stray items rolling along the floor, and held the door open until they trundled out of the café, grateful that her own children were past the having-tantrums-in-public-places stage of life.

"Thanks a lot," said the woman, her eyes brimming with frustration and embarrassment. The circles under them were the bruised blue of Italian plums. "I don't know which is worse: the loneliness of staying home or the humiliation of trying to go out."

"This too shall pass, believe me," Liz said. "My twins were experts at demolition; restaurants practically had to renovate after we ate there. But now that they are teenagers, they are almost civilized."

The woman laughed, preoccupied with steering her stroller around a bicycle locked to a streetlamp, and Liz slipped away before the conversation could return, as all conversations seemed to these days, to the body in the park.

ENTERING HER SHOP, SHE found herself inadvertently locking the door instead of opening up for business. Ever since she had found James Scott's body, she'd been taking refuge in books again the way she did as a girl. Like many lonely children, Liz had been convinced that she belonged elsewhere and reading inspired the hope that she might discover her own secret power by walking through a wardrobe or rubbing an old amulet. In fact, the power of books was twofold: not only did they transport her to a better world, but while she was reading she couldn't possibly be expected to do anything else. Her mother might complain about how messy her room was and her father might suggest that she ought to be playing outdoors, but generally their nagging ceased when they saw her with her nose in a book. So finding sanctuary among her beloved volumes was familiar.

The panic behind it, however, was not. Like the smell of James Scott's dead body, it had seeped into everything.

The bookstore had its own characteristic aroma, musty and leathery at the same time and, despite an unfortunate hint of mildew, Liz had always thought of it as the smell of knowledge. She inhaled deeply, hoping to drive the miasma of death from her nostrils, but it persisted like a malicious rumour. She needed to distract herself. Luckily there was always a lot of work to do in the shop; she could change the window display or dust books, read library journals or online reviews, file papers or, if all else failed, pay a few overdue bills.

In order to avoid the more tedious chores and to keep her mind occupied, Liz decided to rearrange her three tables — which were currently devoted to biography, fiction, and children's literature — thematically. She decided that the first table would display books relating to food (cookbooks mainly, but also *Green Eggs and Ham, Like Water for Chocolate, The Debt to Pleasure, The Edible Woman, Stanley Park, Kitchen, Bread and Wine, The Asparagus Feast, Ice Cream*), the second should be about animals (a lot of non-fiction, many beautifully illustrated children's picture books, and *The Moon by Whale Light, My Family and Other Animals, White Fang, Animal Farm, Shakespeare's Dog, The Trumpet of the Swan, Watership Down, Life of Pi, Elephant Winter, The White Bone*), and the third about shelter (big coffee-table tomes about decorating, home renovation and architecture, *To the Lighthouse, A House is a House for Me, Little House on the Prairie, A House for Mr. Biswas, Jalna, Anne of Green Gables, Wuthering Heights, Bleak House, The House of Mirth, The House on Mango Street, Housekeeping, Middlemarch, Northanger Abbey, House of*

Orphans, As For Me and My House, Howards End, The House of the Spirits).

The last table was the hardest to curate. Eventually Liz had to stop piling up titles because there wasn't enough room. It was amazing how many books told the history of a single building, identifying its fate with that of its inhabitants. Of course, traditionally the word "house" referred not only to a building but also to a dynasty like The House of Atreus or The House of Bourbon or even, God help us, The House of Windsor. In *The Fall of the House of Usher,* Edgar Allan Poe made the metaphor literal: when the last heir died of guilt and grief, the building itself collapsed. These days, people rarely stayed in the place where they grew up. Even in England, most hereditary mansions had been turned into museums — a couple of which she'd dragged her own reluctant children around on a much-anticipated and vaguely disappointing visit "home."

Canada did not have the same tradition of landed gentry. The closest thing to the family estate over here was usually a ramshackle cottage with a few feet of rocky waterfront. Lumpy bunk beds, a cribbage board, a bookcase full of water-damaged Agatha Christies, a canoe, and more mosquitoes than people: if Canadians had a national dream, this was it. Or no, not the cottage itself, but being able to sit on one's dock at sunset listening to the loons calling to each other across the tranquil water. That's what Canadian identity was based on really, not the land that people possessed but the wilderness that no one owned. Though modest when compared to the grandiose self-images of other nations, it was probably something to celebrate in a world where ignorant armies clash by night.

Unfortunately, Liz didn't own a cottage and therefore could never make a patriotic escape to the great outdoors with a two-four of beer on Victoria Day. Most of the people she knew didn't own one either, because — like her — they had come to Toronto from somewhere else, not only from other towns or provinces but — like her — from other countries. And once they got here they kept right on moving, changing residences as their households expanded or contracted. The basic trajectory was familiar: apartment with roommates, apartment with partner or spouse, starter home, family home, empty nest and finally, if you lived long enough, a single room in a nursing home surrounded by more memories than furniture. All modern people were nomads even when they lived in cities.

Thinking about real estate brought her back to James Scott, dispatched so violently in one of the most exclusive neighbour-hoods in the city. Could his profession really have had anything to do with his murder? So many people seemed to think so. That she was preoccupied with houses today suggested that deep down, Liz thought so too.

But she had to get a hold of herself. In two months her mother would be arriving from Prince Edward Island for Christmas, and the last thing Liz wanted was for her to find out that there had been a murder in the neighbourhood — not when she was already in the habit of phoning Liz in a panic whenever she read about any danger in the big bad city. Gang shootings? She called Liz. A five-car pileup on the 401? She called Liz. Blizzards, tornadoes, salmonella outbreaks? She called Liz. During the SARS scare she had been on the phone daily, trying to persuade Liz to grab the children and flee until the plague had dispersed. When Liz laughed off her fears, she kept arguing that at the very least they should all stay huddled indoors together, playing scrabble by candlelight and living off canned goods, donning surgical masks whenever they absolutely had to go outside.

Liz knew she would be alone with her mother most of the time since Josh and Sam had made it clear that they had no intention of spending their holiday listening to Granny's meandering stories about how she met their granddad, whom they had never known. They no longer found it entertaining to help Granny bake her famous shortbread cookies, or put together a thousand-piece jigsaw puzzle, or wind skeins of prickly wool into balls to be knitted into hats and mittens they would never wear after she'd left. But without the distraction provided by the kids, how could she avoid letting something slip about the murder? On the other hand, even if Liz kept quiet, her mother was perceptive enough to recognize that something was wrong because of her changed behaviour. For it had changed, and radically.

Since she found the body, Liz no longer walked Jasper in Wychwood Park or Cedarvale Ravine. Instead, she strolled along St. Clair, dirty and noisy as it was, dodging endless construc- tion and bicycles and beggars, because the bustle of daily commerce made her feel safe. Whereas in the past she just threw a house key in her pocket before she went out, now she had a cellphone with her at all times and called her kids more often than they liked just to check on them. She even gave them extra money for cabs in case of emergency, money she suspected they were spending on cappuccinos after school.

Worst of all, she had developed insomnia. No matter how stressful her life had been before, Elizabeth Ryerson had been a reliable sleeper. Her ability to nod off deeply and gratefully, any time, any place, was her most notorious talent. On lumpy pullout sofa beds and sagging horsehair mattresses, squeezed between fat men on airplanes, in freezing cabins and stuffy tents, she slept. Through morning sickness and breastfeeding twins, through heartbreak and divorce, she slept. But no longer. Now she stayed up all night drinking tea while doing the cryptic crossword or playing Boggle on the computer. Faithful Jasper was compelled to abandon his cozy spot at the end of the bed and follow her from the kitchen table to the dining room sofa and back until close to dawn.

If only for Jasper's sake, Liz needed a resolution. She needed to know what had happened to James Scott, and why. But whatever the police knew they weren't saying, so she determined to buckle down and do some investigating of her own. All those research skills she'd learned at the Faculty of Information Science would finally come in handy. She would find out everything she could about the murdered man: his background, education, his business dealings, his private life. And once she'd proved to herself that his case was exceptional and that her corner of the earth was not permanently tainted, and that she and those she loved were not under threat, her life could resume its natural cadence.

4

"WHERE DO YOU WANT me to put this box?" the UPS guy asked.

"Oh, just dump it on the desk at the back, thanks," said Liz, gesturing vaguely with her chin because her right hand was occupied in signing the delivery form while the left balanced a wobbling stack of books on her canted hip.

The delivery man also had to angle his hips to avoid bumping into her or knocking over books; he was less successful at avoiding Jasper's enthusiastic welcome. Eventually he negotiated his way through the cluttered store and found a few bare inches of wood upon which to unload his burden, lingering long enough to help himself to a fistful of orange and yellow candy corn from the apothecary jar on the desk before leaving.

This candy jar, its contents changing seasonally, was only one of many things about Liz's shop that drove her germ-phobic mother crazy. But to Liz the bookstore was an expression of her personality and she liked candy, especially when she was working. Little jolts of sugar all day long kept her mind sharp and her mood cheerful. In fact, she was happier bustling around the shop than she was at home upstairs. At home she had to do uncongenial work like cooking and cleaning and laundry and ironing; she had to help her kids with schoolwork — well, not so much anymore; grade eleven science and math were beyond her capabilities — and negotiate their extracurricular activities and occasional, very occasional, holidays with their father. At home she felt the full weight of being a single mother with an ex-husband who lived just one floor above her. But not when she was at work; then she wasn't anyone's ex-anything, she was simply "the bookstore lady." And as much as she adored her kids and was proud to be their mother, this was her favourite identity.

Outside of a Dog, despite its eccentric name, was very cozy. Six-foot-high bookshelves lined the walls, except for the big bay window in front where Jasper liked to curl up and another small area along the east wall where there was a working fireplace. A cheerful rug in front of the hearth defined the reading area, which included two rocking chairs, a sofa covered in red plaid and stray dog hair, a basket of wood and newspapers for kindling and another basket full of toys and picture books to occupy the youngest visitors while their adults shopped. Over the mantel hung an assortment of framed book covers and cartoons from *The New Yorker*; along it marched a row of brightly painted Mexican wooden dogs. Liz hadn't wanted to overdo the canine motif, but it was irresistible. These days a store had to have a gimmick to be successful.

Still, Liz flattered herself that the main draw for her customers was not the quirky decor but her own profound knowledge of literature, and the haven she provided for other literate types in the neighbourhood. At occasional intervals along the bookshelves were pinned index cards covered with quotations and book reviews. Some had been written neatly by hand; others were clipped from magazines and newspapers or printed from Internet book blogs. She was responsible for a few, but most were brought in by customers wanting to share their enthusiasms. Other kinds of notices were pinned to the corkboard covering the inside of the front door. These she restricted to local events and causes, including lost cats and/ or free kittens, babysitting, housecleaning services offered or requested, music lessons, church fundraisers, garage sales, and yoga classes.

At the back of the room stood a massive oak desk left over from the space's earlier incarnation as an antique shop. It was big enough to hold a laptop computer, a fax-copier-scanner-printer, an assortment of files, invoices, letters, catalogues and trade magazines, and an overflowing basket of stationery items. Behind it, against the far wall, were a couple of battered filing cabinets and an enormous aquarium housing a tortoise named Darwin — also courtesy of the former tenant — who was taken for a waddle around the store twice a day and sometimes, in fine weather, to the park. The rest of the space included a utilitarian bathroom, a storage area, and a small kitchen. Liz liked to provide food and drink at poetry readings, book launches, and the monthly in-house book club but was wary of spills on her merchandise, so she tried to confine the eating to the back of the shop. That most of her books were second-hand made her job more relaxed, since nobody expected used books to be in pristine condition. She kept the more valuable first editions locked up in a special glass showcase, out of harm's way.

Not that she had many first editions. Liz Ryerson wasn't a collector of books or indeed of anything else. She had never managed to hang on to her own favourite volumes, compulsively giving them away to whomever she felt needed to read them. Probably that was the main reason she ended up as the proprietor of a bookstore: she loved matching people to literature. Sometimes she jokingly called herself a Doctor of Letters, since she could prescribe a book for any taste or occasion. And, after all, it was through books that she had made a life for herself. Timid as a child, lonely as a teenager, hardworking and solitary — at first — in library school, Liz had come out of her shell once she discovered that her passion for books was shared by more people than she had realized. And with that discovery came another: that she herself had an untapped capacity for gregariousness and a gift for witty conversation. She'd always loved words on the page, but living in that quiet house with a grimly clenched mother, a mostly absent father, and a big brother obsessed with sports, she'd never realized how much fun talking could be.

She had become so chatty that her children didn't believe she had been shy at their age; they frequently demanded confirmation from their granny — or as frequently as they could, since they didn't see her very often, now that family vacations at the beach were a thing of the past. Liz's mother did not answer her grandchildren's questions with the kind of illustrative detail they were hoping for. They could start off a sentence for her to fill in but rarely were satisfied with the answer. "When she was little, Mum was so shy that ..." Sammy might begin, but Granny would conclude simply "she was afraid to raise her hand in class," or "she didn't bring any friends home from school," but then add that she had been the same way herself as a child so it wasn't surprising, and that her grandchildren must have got their fearlessness from the other side of the family. At which point Liz would have to intervene, to keep her mother from expanding upon this observation with some comment about "Jewish boldness" that verged perilously on anti-Semitism. Though Mrs. Ryerson had long ago accepted Adam Silver, and by extension his large and voluble extended family, she'd never quite managed to overcome the prejudices she'd grown up with, and since the divorce she felt less inhibited about expressing them.

Liz sighed. Everyone she knew had problems with their mothers. Presumably her own kids would be complaining about her one day, no matter how hard she tried to be fair to them.

The bell tied to the front door jingled. She looked up. A man was giving his big black umbrella a good shake on the doorstep before folding it up neatly and entering the shop. He was altogether a neat person, with his belted raincoat and plaid scarf, his grey hair cut short, and his beard and moustache trimmed precisely.

"Hello," he said. "Do you remember me? Maxime Bertrand."

"We met when I was out walking the dog, right?"

"That's right. In fact, I came here to bring him a treat. I made a pot of soup yesterday and had a juicy marrowbone left over."

"That was so thoughtful of you. Jasper, come see what nice Monsieur Bertrand brought." The dog needed no encouragement; he was already on his way over, tail wagging and nose twitching in anticipation.

"Call me Max, please."

"Okay. And you can call me Liz. By the way, you now have a friend for life," Liz observed, as Jasper took the big round bone delicately between his teeth and lay down under her desk to savour it.

"Do you have any good murder mysteries?"

"You bet. There's a whole section against the far wall there: Reginald Hill, Laurie King, Peter Robinson, Michael Dibdin, P.D. James, and my personal favourite, Kate Atkinson. There might even be some Simenon or Fred Vargas in French if you look hard enough. Maybe I should be reading those books myself, now that I think about it."

"Why do you say that?"

"Well, I stumbled over a dead body right after I met you last week."

"Good Lord. I can't believe it. In this neighbourhood?"

"I can't believe it either. And I can't believe that I just said 'dead body' — how redundant is that? It's like saying 'free gift,' which is another expression I hate." She laughed, but her laughter sounded shrill and forced, even to herself.

Max looked at her with concern. "You know, I may be wrong, but I don't remember noticing those dark shadows under your eyes when we first met. Are you feeling all right?"

"I am having a little trouble sleeping," she confessed. "The experience was pretty disturbing. But probably what upset me the most is that it happened in Wychwood Park, where I used to walk my dog every day. I feel like the place is polluted now."

"Death is everywhere, all the time, whether we are aware of it or not. To quote Horace, 'Pale Death with impartial tread beats at the poor man's cottage door and at the palaces of kings.'"

"But this time Pale Death wasn't impartial, was he? Dying may be natural, but surely murder is not."

"That's debatable, Liz. People can be very violent."

"I know that in theory, but my own family was so British and buttoned-up and I've spent most of my life hiding in books. I guess fate decreed it was time for me to face reality."

"Nonsense. It was just a case of your being in the wrong place at the wrong time," he objected.

"Maybe, Max. But what's worse is that I knew the guy. Not well, but he was a real estate agent I consulted just a couple of months ago. My ex-husband wanted to know the value of this building; we own it together, it's kind of a long story. Anyway, I keep seeing his face in front of me and wanting to reach out and warn him."

"I can imagine."

"I've been researching the guy on the Internet, trying to find clues as to why he was killed. It's ridiculous, but I can't help myself."

"It's not at all ridiculous. I'm just like you. When my wife was dying I practically became a medical student looking for a cure for her. Research made me feel that I was doing something useful, and at the same time it distracted me from my grief."

"Thank you for understanding. And for indulging me. I'm sure what you went through with your wife was a thousand times worse than my silly obsession with this business." She sighed and then said hesitantly, "It's weird. You're the first person I've actually confided in and I don't know you."

"That's why you can talk to me," he replied, smiling. "It would be even easier if we were strangers on a train, destined never to see each other again. But I intend to become a loyal customer, so you will have to see me again whether or not you want to."

"Well, all my loyal customers join me in a cup of tea. Will you? I really need it, after pouring out my heart like that."

"I would love a cup of tea, thank you."

Jasper followed them to the kitchen at the back of the store and flopped down beside Max's chair to gnaw on his marrow-bone. His contented sounds filled the room while the kettle boiled and Liz rummaged around for some cookies.

"Something just occurred to me, Liz," Max said suddenly. "Do you know whether the murder was actually committed in Wychwood Park? Maybe the body was just dumped there because it was a convenient hiding place."

"I never thought of that."

"Would it make you feel better if you found out that the man was killed somewhere else?"

"Probably." Liz thought for a moment, running virtual electrodes over her own skull, gauging her responses to this alternative interpretation of events. "Yes, you're absolutely right, it would."

"Well, then, we'll have to uncover the whole story before deciding that this neighbourhood is going to the dogs. As it were. Sorry, Jasper," he laughed.

"We? As in you and I?" Liz asked, swirling boiling water around in the teapot to warm it up.

"Why not? I'm retired and as I told you, a widower. I could use a new project to keep me busy. And to quote Horace again, 'Your own safety is at stake when your neighbour's wall is ablaze.'"

"What did you do before you retired?" Liz asked curiously.

"I was a professor of Classics."

"I should have guessed. Most people don't go around quoting Horace these days."

"Alas, no," he conceded, smiling. "What about you? Have you always sold books?"

"No, but I've always worked with them. I was trained as a librarian."

"Perfect," he exclaimed. "We'll make an excellent team."

"I would have thought we would make a pretty feeble one," Liz said, putting two mugs in front of them.

"Not at all. We both have curiosity, research skills, endless patience, a wide knowledge of things past and present, and no vanity. What more could a couple of private investigators need?"

"I can think of lots of things, starting with experience. A few muscles would be nice, or maybe even a gun. Not that I'd ever have the nerve to shoot one. Which is why I'd make such a pathetic detective in the first place."

"Nonsense, my dear. Remember what Hercule Poirot always says? To solve a crime all that is required is the operation of 'the little grey cells,' and between us, despite my failing memory, I'm sure we have more than the average number of those."

He paused to sip his tea, then dipped a ginger snap in it before taking an appreciative bite. "Ginger is supposed to be good for the memory, did you know that?"

"I thought that was ginseng."

"It might be. I don't remember," he said, and they both laughed.

HE STAYED in the small-town jail for more than a week until they could send him to a bigger town with a bigger jail where boys and men were properly segregated. The drunk was released right away, so at least he had the cell to himself, which was some kind of good luck. Still, there was nothing to do but lie on his cot, wondering what would happen next. The police eventually tracked down his real mother and called her. He begged her to come see him; he told her how frightened he was and how much he missed her. She just sobbed that this was all her fault while, in the background, he could hear her boyfriend shouting that the little bastard got what he deserved. After the phone went dead he sat there, waiting, for at least an hour, but his mother never called back.

He languished in the new jail for six months until his trial date was set. And in all that time he said nothing to anybody about the fire, except that he was sorry. Mostly he cried, stared at the wall, and slept. A teacher visited a couple of times a week to make sure he didn't fall behind too much in school. While she was there he did a bunch of math sheets and drew maps; he read stories and answered questions about them. His work was quite neat and the teacher complimented him on his good attitude. But as soon as she left, he went back to sleep, ignoring the textbooks she left behind to keep him occupied.

He was offered legal aid; he was asked if he had any other family he wished to call, any adult relatives who could help him; he was advised that it would be in his best interest to be interviewed by a psychiatrist. But to every suggestion he shook his head no. No, he didn't have anyone to call; no, he didn't want to talk to a therapist; no, no one could help him.

Yes, he was guilty.

5

L IZ AND MAX SPENT most of the afternoon going over the
information she'd found on the late James Scott. This didn't
amount to very much, unfortunately. The man had undoubtedly
been successful in business, his handsome face smiling from
newsletters and brochures as he clutched certificates and trophies
or shook hands with developers and other prominent citizens,
but he kept his private life private. Where he came from, where
he had been educated, what he'd done before joining the real
estate agency, whether he was married or had children, his
hobbies: none of this was floating around in cyberspace.

Popular wisdom to the contrary, it simply wasn't true that
everyone's personal details were accessible to any hack with
a computer and a high speed connection. Liz had already

discovered this when — because of her degree in information science and the assumption that therefore she must be a technical wizard — she was asked to track down her former classmates for her tenth high-school reunion. A surprising number of people had sailed off the map into parts unknown and, despite her best efforts, she had failed to discover their whereabouts. The fact that so many others would not be attending the event had served as a good excuse for her to decline her own invitation, though she would not have attended in any case.

She explained her difficulties in researching James Scott's life to Max as they pursued their elusive quarry. Somehow, in the process, they became friends.

Though Liz was disappointed that she had been unable to discover any substantial information, Max was not. He was excited at the prospect of doing some old-fashioned sleuthing; he couldn't wait to interview suspects and to go looking for clues. He declared that the only way to find a killer was to find out who had motive, means, and opportunity, and none of these crucial factors were apt to reveal themselves on a digital screen.

"You're joking, right?" asked Liz.

"Not in the least."

"But we don't have any suspects, Max."

"On the contrary, we have too many. We just need to narrow them down. Now, one thing I learned from teaching university is that academics love to complain about their colleagues. Under their good manners and phony English accents, most of them are just seething with suppressed envy and resentment."

"I know what you mean," Liz laughed. "My ex-husband teaches photography at the art college and half the people in his department are walking around with invisible knives sticking out of their backs."

"So," continued Max, "assuming that things are not significantly different in any other profession, we need to ferret out a few discontented real estate agents to give us the dirt on James Scott."

"But Max, why would anyone confide in us? We're not the police."

"We could pretend to be thinking of buying or selling real estate, then gently steer the conversation in the direction of the crime."

"I can't. Adam and I co-own this property and because he wants to sell it and I don't, pretending I was considering a move would make my life ridiculously complicated."

"But I'm just renting my apartment and charming though it is, suddenly I find it doesn't suit me," Max said with a grin. "I miss having a garden, for one thing — retired people need healthy hobbies and nothing is healthier than gardening. As Cicero says, 'Anyone who has a library and a garden wants for nothing.'"

"You've got to love that Cicero. And any man who can quote him so aptly."

"Thank you, on both our behalves. So, my dear, I wonder if you could find it in your heart to help a poor doddering old man find a reliable real estate agent?"

LIZ WISHED SHE HAD asked the agent to come to her place, since accompanying Max to the agency and back, as well as sitting through what promised to be a lengthy interview, was going to take at least two hours. If they'd been at the bookstore she could have kept busy behind the scenes and let Max do all the talking. She could even have taken notes while eavesdropping. But in this impersonal room, with its minimalist furniture and tasteful posters of Toronto doorways, she felt as helpless as if she were waiting for a root canal at the dentist.

There was nothing to read except promotional materials featuring preposterously expensive properties, and nothing to do but try to look sincere. Pretending to be what she was not wasn't easy for Liz. Despite her capacious memory she'd never had good roles in school plays because she was unable to imagine being someone else. In her darker moments, she wondered if this was evidence not of a robust sense of identity but the contrary: she couldn't imitate other people because she didn't know who she was herself. In addition, she was exceptionally clumsy, all knees and elbows, prone to knocking things over onstage and getting unintentional laughs. So usually she ended up being the prompter.

Max, on the other hand, was clearly enjoying himself. His accent, ordinarily slight, had become much more pronounced — or maybe her attention had been drawn to it by the beret he had perched jauntily on one side of his head, and the flamboyance of the gestures that accompanied his every comment. All he needed was a Gauloise smouldering between his fingers and a glass of red wine on the table in front of him to complete the picture.

"I have come here from Montréal," he declared, which was technically true, although his journey west on Highway 401 had taken place at least thirty years earlier. "But now my daughter wishes to join me and the space I have rented is, alas" — here he staged a deep sigh — "not big enough. This is why I have decided to buy a house."

"Traditionally, as you know," the agent replied, "Toronto real estate has proved to be a very good investment. Although I have to say that Montreal has always been my favourite Canadian city."

"You are obviously a lady of the good taste. We shall work well together," he replied, leaning toward her with a smile that could melt permafrost.

"I certainly hope so, Monsieur Bertrand. Now, tell me more about what exactly you are looking for."

In a navy blue pantsuit accented by a brilliantly coloured silk scarf and gold hoop earrings that she hoped hinted at the sensual vagabond under her staid, career-woman exterior, Annette Horvath appeared utterly smitten by Maxime and oblivious to Liz, which was a good thing, since the latter was about to explode from suppressed laughter.

"I am looking for a charming small house, conveniently located, with a fenced backyard to keep safe a dog, also small. My daughter is most attached to her dog."

"How many bedrooms do you want?"

"Three, I think, will be sufficient. One for me, *évidemment*, one for Chantal, and one for when we have the guests."

"Do you care whether it is detached or not?"

Liz felt guilty to see the woman earnestly taking notes but consoled herself with the thought that prospective clients must occasionally change their minds, so she and Max would not be the first people to waste Mrs. Horvath's time.

"I care only that it is quiet."

"Well then, detached is best. Though I must warn you, you will have to pay quite a bit more."

"It seems I will have to pay quite a bit whatever I buy, no?" he replied, with an exaggerated shrug. "The market is, how you say, very hot."

"Yes indeed," she laughed, finally catching Liz's eye as if to say, "isn't he delightful."

Liz was worried that Max might be overdoing the whole Gallic charm routine, and decided it was time for her to intervene.

"Maxime had hoped to move into my neighbourhood," she said. "Hillcrest Village."

"But now I am not so sure," he interrupted, "now that there has been a murder in the *quartier*. Chantal will not want to move to somewhere so dangerous. Her dog Charlot, he is not very fierce."

"Hillcrest is an extremely safe neighbourhood," the agent said quickly. "I can show you municipal crime statistics broken down by area and you will see that it ranks very low both in crimes against people and crimes against property."

"Nonetheless, a man has been killed," Max objected.

"Well, things like that never happen normally," she protested, a red flush creeping up her face to match the artful rouge on her cheekbones.

"Would you feel safe moving there yourself, Mrs. Horvath?" Liz asked.

"Please call me Annette. And yes, I would move to Hillcrest in a minute. I wouldn't be at all worried."

"Then Maxime, maybe you don't need to worry either," said Liz. Now they were getting somewhere.

"But the dead man, was he not in your *métier*?" Max asked, recognizing his cue.

"Yes, he was. In fact, believe it or not, he worked right here."

"Really!" said Liz, hoping she sounded convincingly surprised. "I'm so sorry; I had no idea. Was he a friend of yours?"

"Not really, but I've been at this office for the last two years so obviously I saw quite a bit of him."

"That he was murdered suggests he was not someone a lovely lady like you would wish to be friends with," Max asserted. "He must have been a gambler, or perhaps a user of the drugs."

"Good heavens, no," the agent said hastily. "Mr. Scott was very polite and hardworking. He was one of our most popular agents, in fact."

"What made him so popular?" Liz asked.

"He had an encyclopedic knowledge of the city and knew all the sales figures past and present."

"Was he married?"

"No. Actually, now that I think of it, he never even brought a date to company events. Which is kind of odd when you think about it, since most of the folks in this business are really extroverted. You have to be, to spend all day driving around in your car with strangers."

"But Monsieur Scott was not so friendly?" Max asked.

"He wasn't unfriendly. He was just really private."

"My goodness, half the people in Toronto are like that these days; that's life in the big city, isn't it?" said Liz, concerned that the focus of their investigation was becoming a little too obvious.

"But Madame Annette, if he was *un bonhomme ordinaire*,

why did somebody decide to murder him?" Max continued, unperturbed.

"I'm sure it was just bad luck. A robbery gone wrong, or something like that. Now, why don't I get us some coffee and then we can look through the listings for your area? How do you take it?"

"With milk, thanks," said Liz.

"Black, two sugars," said Maxime. "You are very kind. *Merci.*"

"I'll be right back." Annette Horvath almost ran from the room, clearly anxious to change the subject from the grisly murder of a colleague to the more profitable and less distressing topic of home ownership.

"Max, I don't mean to be critical, you're absolutely amazing," Liz whispered, "but you might want to tone down your Maurice Chevalier shtick a little."

"Really? But *la belle dame*, she is eating it up, no?"

"For now. But she might catch on."

"Anyhow, I don't think Madame Horvath is going to prove all that useful," said Maxime thoughtfully. "She's much too nice. We need to find someone jealous of James Scott's success, someone who would be willing to, how you say, spill the *haricots*."

"Hmm," Liz replied. "I would have thought the kind of beans you can spill were called *fèves*. But I think you're right."

THEY LEFT THE OFFICE with a pile of facts and figures as well as the most profound gratitude that they didn't really need somewhere to live. Liz couldn't imagine having to pay the kind of prices people were asking for narrow three-bedroom, semi-detached houses with unfinished basements and no parking; she couldn't imagine moving at all, ever, anywhere, although Adam was itching to go off somewhere on his own. He'd been making noises about it for some time.

"So what do we know now that we didn't know before?" she asked Maxime, as they hopped onto the streetcar. "Besides the fact that under that dignified exterior, you are an incorrigible ham? That is to say, a *jambon*."

"Most academics are frustrated actors," Maxime countered mildly. "We all love a captive audience."

"I guess so. But in the theatre, the audience gets to decide whether you are any good or not. If memory serves, I had an awful lot of teachers at university who would have been booed off the legitimate stage."

"Which is precisely why they were hiding in the ivory tower. There is no audience so appreciative as one dependent upon you for grades."

"Humph," said Liz. "Did you realize that I actually said 'humph'? Usually when I read that in a novel, I think to myself, 'Nobody ever says that in real life,' but I just did."

"Which is why reading is so good for you. It expands your vocabulary."

"Okay, Max, let's get serious. I left my assistant Georgia in charge of the bookstore this morning and I need to get back to save it from her. She's been trying to persuade me to decorate the place for Hallowe'en with flying witches and smoking cauldrons and God knows what other kitschy stuff. I'm dreading what she might do if left unsupervised for too long. So we'd better have learned something useful on this little expedition."

"We learned that James Scott was a very private individual."

"Yes."

"And we learned that this is unusual, since real estate agents tend to be gregarious."

"That's not much to go on, is it?"

"Perhaps it is more than it appears to be," Max said slowly. "This murder may have been entirely random, in which case the victim's character was irrelevant. But if it was not random everything we learn about James Scott is useful. Especially things that make him unusual."

"Maybe. But only if you conclude that instead of him being murdered because he sold crappy houses at inflated prices to desperate people, he was murdered because he wasn't very chatty."

"Or maybe he was murdered for the same reason that he wasn't very chatty."

"Which was what?" asked Liz, mystified.

"Which was that he had something to hide."

LIZ INSISTED THAT MAX head straight home because she really needed to go to work. She felt the familiar sensation of comfort as she entered the store. Jasper loped over to greet her, his tail a blur of happiness. Georgia was all smiles. Despite Liz's nervousness, she had not redecorated ghoulishly, nor had she rearranged the window display or invited buskers inside to entertain the customers. She had, however, sold a copy of *What to Expect When You're Expecting* to a grandmother-to-be who was almost hyperventilating with excitement, a vegan cookbook to a cadaverous man who looked like he'd be better off eating a double cheeseburger, and a Spanish-English dictionary to a couple taking an impromptu Costa Rican vacation. Georgia recounted these exploits with amazement because she rarely sold anything to anybody. Her numerous piercings and tattoos, which Josh and Samantha envied loudly and often in support of their ongoing campaign for equivalent bodily adornment, tended to inhibit some of Liz's less adventurous clientele. This was unfortunate, since Georgia was an avid and discerning reader and as harmless as a hedgehog under that spiky exterior.

Suggesting that Georgia take a break by walking Jasper around the block, Liz settled in behind her desk with a huge sigh of relief. This is where she belonged, embraced by lots and lots of lovely books, not chasing shadows. Especially homicidal shadows armed with blunt objects. She was starting to feel silly pretending to be a detective, but how could she quit the game without letting Maxime down? He was really having fun, probably the most fun he'd had in a long time. Maybe she could encourage him to continue on his own so that she could play an obsequious Dr. Watson to his Sherlock Holmes? That way she could still exercise her curiosity without jeopardizing her business, which was only marginally profitable at the best of times, as evidenced by today's post. As usual, it consisted mostly of bills. She kicked off her shoes and settled in to sort it into three trays labelled "pay now," "pay later," and "ignore for as long as possible."

There was nothing else of interest except the new *Quill & Quire*; everything else was junk mail: a takeout menu from a

Chinese restaurant, solicitations from contractors and politicians promising extraordinary service and competitive prices, and flyers from real estate agents boasting about their success. She was sweeping the whole pile into the recycling bin when she realized that the glossiest of the flyers, the one with good quality photographs in full colour and tasteful typography, had been sent to her by none other than the late James Scott himself.

Liz shivered. It was disconcerting to be greeted from beyond the grave by a smiling murder victim trying to sell you a house. Clearly the situation called for a sardonic pun about "buying the farm" or "going to one's heavenly mansion," but she didn't have the heart for wordplay today.

Why hadn't they cancelled the distribution of the flyers? Could the real estate agency have forgotten all about them? That didn't seem likely. Probably what happened was the flyers had already been printed up at great expense and nobody wanted to waste them. After all, they could still attract prospective customers even if the agent himself was no longer available. Maybe the fact that he had been murdered would even lure additional customers: the kind of ghouls who are obsessed with dead celebrities.

Liz stared curiously at the smiling face on the flyer. She'd always thought her ex-husband Adam was attractive, but this guy was off the charts. He was fair-skinned, with bright blue eyes and thick dark hair: a combination of features her mother called "Black Irish," and attributed to assignations between local colleens and Spanish sailors who washed up on the shores of Ireland after the Elizabethan navy sunk their Armada. Liz wasn't sure there was any historical basis for this story, but it was so delightful she'd always chosen to believe it. Of course, the man's last name had been "Scott," which made an Irish origin seem unlikely. But then again — if she remembered her university course on the history of the British Isles correctly — a lot of the religious conflict in Ireland began with the arrival of Presbyterians from the Scottish Lowlands, so why couldn't there be Irishmen named Scott?

In spite of her resolution to stop snooping, Liz's mania for historical accuracy was irresistible. Moreover, reading something, anything at all, was invariably her recourse when she was upset. So she switched on her laptop. A couple of minutes on the Internet rewarded her with the surprising and utterly delightful fact that the name "Scott" actually means "Irishman" in Latin. Apparently, in the sixth century, the Irish had colonized the north of Britain. Probably Maxime could have told her this, being a classical scholar; she would have to ask him the next time she saw him. Still, she doubted that this nugget of etymology, though exactly the kind of fundamentally useless trivia that delighted her, had any relevance whatsoever to their investigation. No, not their investigation; his investigation. She had promised herself she was going to give it up.

Names were often confusing. Sometimes Liz regretted having named her daughter Samantha because the inevitable nickname "Sam" meant the girl was usually expected to be a boy. It was even worse given that she was a twin: "Josh" and "Sam" sounded like a pair of identical brothers, mini-Huckleberry Finns with freckles and slingshots, instead of the combative opposites they really were: she short, dark, and fierce and he tall, blond, and affable. Samantha took after Adam's family while Joshua was the spitting image of her own father at that age. Of course, there was no genetic reason they should look more alike than any other brother and sister just because they were born at the same time. There really ought to be a better term for non-identical twins than fraternal, given that Sam wasn't actually a boy. And what if her twins had both been girls, which the law of averages suggested they must be at least one-quarter of the time. Wouldn't that have been even more confusing?

She was rescued from this profitless line of speculation by the return of Georgia and Jasper, the former bearing a Styrofoam container of sushi and a large bottle of green tea, the latter greeting her as though they had been separated for several days rather than a few minutes.

"Since you don't appear to be working anyway, Liz, how about some lunch?" her assistant asked dryly.

"I was just sorting today's mail and then I was really, truly, absolutely positively going to buckle down and pay some bills. But I admit it, boss, you caught me daydreaming," Liz replied. "About names, actually. Are you ever mistaken for a man? I mean, do people sometimes expect a George instead of a Georgia?"

"Pretty often."

"Does it bother you?"

"No, being ambiguous when it comes to gender is my religion. If Ruby and I ever have kids, we're going to give them unisex names on purpose."

"Like Chris? Or Pat? Or Alex?"

"Sorry, nicknames are cheating. I mean names that are androgynous in their original form. Names like Sasha, or Robin, or Adrian, or Skye."

"Sasha's actually a nickname, my dear. It's the Russian short form for Alexander."

"Not in Toronto, it isn't. In Toronto it's the name of every second toddler in the sandbox."

"How would you know?"

"Ruby has a lot of married colleagues. Married colleagues who insist on having their offspring join us at dinner to demonstrate their ethnically diverse palates and all-around cuteness."

"I get the picture," Liz smiled. "I suspect Adam and I were just as obnoxious back in the day."

"Were?" said Georgia.

"Point taken," Liz replied. "Still, despite my irritating adoration of my own children, I'm surprised that you're choosing names for those you don't even have yet. Isn't that kind of, I don't know, bourgeois?"

"Maybe," Georgia retorted. "But it's not like I've planned my wedding or anything."

"No white gown for you, I suppose?"

"Let's not even go there," Georgia snorted. "Unless I could accessorize with Doc Martens and black fishnet stockings."

"What does Ruby think?"

"Dr. Ruby Leung would marry me tomorrow and move to the suburbs, I swear. You have no idea how conventional that girl is, deep down. All she really wants to do is bake cookies and slipcover the furniture. Her secret role model is not Marie Curie but Martha Stewart."

They were both screaming with laughter at the image of Georgia's partner — an internationally respected expert in human genetics — as a domestic goddess, when the telephone rang.

"Outside of a Dog Rare and Used Books," Liz sang into the mouthpiece. "Liz Ryerson speaking."

"Hi, Liz, it's me: Adam. We need to talk."

"Now? I just got back to work, Adam; I was out all morning. Is it important?"

"Very."

"Oh my God, did the school call? Is something wrong with one of the kids? Why didn't you ring me earlier? I had my cell-phone with me. I even remembered to charge it today!"

"No, no, don't worry, it's nothing like that," he said sooth-ingly. "I said it was important, not that it was an emergency."

"Then can't it wait until after work?" she said, with a sigh of relief.

"Sure, but I may be back kind of late. I have a meeting."

"Adam, do you do any actual teaching at that place? It seems like all you ever have is meetings."

"This one is important. We're choosing sabbatical replacements for next year."

"Practically no teaching, just the occasional meeting, and then sabbaticals as a reward. What a hard life you have, Professor Silver."

"You can't imagine the drudgery," he said, laughing.

Liz had always loved Adam's laugh. Listening to it, she almost forgot why she kicked him out. "Just knock on my door when you get back," she said.

"Won't the kids be home? I'd rather talk to you in private," he said.

"Sam has a swim meet after school," Liz said, thinking. "I don't remember what Josh is doing. Probably volleyball or band practice. But he never comes home before suppertime anyway."

"All right. Hopefully we'll get a moment alone." He hung up without saying goodbye. Liz listened to the dial tone, her skin prickling with apprehension. Adam had sounded like he was holding something back.

"What was that all about?" asked Georgia, daintily licking a few grains of rice from her fingers.

"I have no idea. But clearly this is going to be a very long day. You may as well go now, Georgie-girl; you did a stellar job this morning, but there isn't much for you to do now."

"Okey-dokey. See you later, my darlings."

Georgia blew a kiss from the door and was gone. Jasper, whose idea of heaven was a perpetual party with everybody he loved in the same room feeding him surreptitious hors d'oeuvres, whimpered a little before settling down with his heavy head on Liz's foot. Why did people always leave? What place could they possibly go that was better than being with him?

Liz felt like lying down on the floor next to him and whimpering too. Whatever his faults as a husband — and they were legion, and mostly female — Adam had never been histrionic, so if he said something was important, she was inclined to believe him. But she didn't think she had the strength to deal with anything else consequential today. Her life, which felt improvisational at the best of times, had gone seriously off script. She was supposed to be a mousy little librarian: a finder of misfiled reference books, not of mouldering corpses. Since she had discovered the body in Wychwood Park she felt that all her safety lay here, in this very space. And if Adam wasn't calling about the kids, he must be calling about the building.

6

WAITING FOR ADAM TO show up, Liz found herself too restless to read and too nervous to do the crossword puzzle, so she decided to clean out the fridge. There were a lot of vegetables turning to mush at the bottom of the bin; this gave her a perfect incentive to make soup. In order to keep busy, she decided to make the soup as elaborate as possible, which meant something curried, with the curry created from scratch. First she crushed cardamom pods, coriander, fennel, and cumin seeds, black peppercorns, cinnamon, and turmeric in a lava stone mortar she and Adam had brought back from a holiday in Mexico. It was the last holiday they'd had alone, the last holiday before the twins were born, before she even knew she was pregnant. In the throes of unsuspected morning sickness cunningly disguising itself as traveller's tummy, unable to eat anything but frozen-fruit-on-a-stick and those crusty white buns the locals called *bolillos*, she hadn't been able to imagine ever wanting to cook again, but Adam — who liked odd tools — bought it anyway. As it turned out, she used the mortar more than he did, so he'd let her keep it. Sometimes she appreciated the opportunity to smash something, even a few innocent bits of twig and seed, especially as the kitchen smelled heavenly afterwards.

It smelled even better after she browned ginger, garlic, and leeks in olive oil and then added carrots and squash, the curry powder, some organic vegetable broth, and her secret ingredient: a splash of orange juice. By the time the soup was ready, the counters and cooktop wiped clean, the chopping board and knives washed and draining in the rack, Adam had arrived, and she felt calm enough to face whatever he had to tell her. After accepting a glass of Sauvignon Blanc and a bowl of the soup garnished with a dollop of yogurt and a leaf of cilantro, he reminded her that he had been planning a half-sabbatical in the New Year; he had come to tell her that he would be away travelling for part of it.

"Where are you going?" Liz asked politely, relieved that this was his big news. She could deal with Adam going away. Though the kids would miss him and there might be times when she might want to consult him about something or other, not running into his girlfriends for a while might be peaceful.

"Southeast Asia," he said.

"That sounds exciting." They had often talked about going on a really big trip once the kids had grown up and they were free again. She experienced a flare of grief, realizing Adam would be achieving this goal without her, but quickly doused the unwanted flame in a sip of wine.

"Yeah. Laura is really thrilled. She's never gone anywhere so far away."

"Lah-oh-ra?" It irritated Liz no end, the way he drew out the name so lovingly. Like the arbitrary Toronto habit of pronouncing "Chile" with a Latin American accent, when "Espagna" remained Spain and "Italia," Italy. It also annoyed her that she'd assumed naively, if only for a nanosecond, that Adam would be travelling alone.

"My girlfriend, the dancer. Remember? You met her when we were bicycling to High Park the last weekend before school started. Josh asked you for some extra granola bars because, as usual, he didn't think we packed enough lunch for him."

He wasn't meeting her eye. Clearly there was a lot more going on with this "Lah-oh-ra" than just a vacation.

"Dark hair? Brazilian? Little gold stud in the side of her nose?" It took remarkable forbearance but she didn't mention the girl's youth or her gorgeous figure.

"Yes. That's her."

"You guys must be getting serious." Was she hallucinating or was he almost purring with pleasure?

"That's what I need to talk to you about, Liz. We're going to be gone for three months, so I told Laura she could move her stuff into my flat. It doesn't make any sense for her to keep paying rent the whole time we're away."

"Well, I guess not. But then ..."

"But then when we get back, we're planning to find a bigger place together."

Her instincts had been right. It was an emergency about the house after all.

"What will you do with your flat, Adam?" Liz asked. She felt sick and dizzy. The wine — a respectable bottle, more expensive than she usually bought — had turned to acid in her belly.

"If I could afford to keep it as a studio and live somewhere else with Laura that would be ideal, but even then I would have to pull my financial stake out of the bookstore. We have to start looking for another partner for you."

"Do you really think it will be easy to find anyone reckless enough to invest in a bookstore?" She couldn't hold back her bitterness.

"I have no idea. But neither do you, since you've never tried."

"I thought you liked living here." She hoped she wasn't whining.

"I did, but the kids finish high school next year and, anyway, they don't need us as much as they did when they were little. You should be thinking about what's next for you, too."

"Don't tell me what I should do, Adam," she snapped. "You gave up that privilege a long time ago."

Responding to the rising tension in the room, Jasper started to growl, and then stood up and walked over to Liz. She stroked him, trying to regain her equilibrium. Patting dogs was supposed to lower your blood pressure, as well as providing comfort for elderly shut-ins and emotionally starved women like her. The way things were going, she was going to need more than poor Jasper to keep her company. Clearly she was destined to spend her dotage in a tiny apartment stinking of tuna and kitty litter.

"Fine. Be like that. But, seriously, Liz, you need to find another partner for the shop. The sooner the better."

Adam rinsed out his bowl and wineglass and put them in the dishwasher, shoved his arms into his black leather jacket, wound a long scarf a couple of times around his neck, and turned to go. Just then Sam flung the door open. Her long hair was wet, her duffle coat unbuttoned, her pretty olive-skinned face glowing.

"Hi, Mum, hi, Dad," she screeched. "I won the freestyle! And my team won the relay as well."

"That's great, Sammy," Adam said, "but you have to start drying your hair before you leave the pool. It's getting cold outside now."

"It takes too long. I can't be bothered," she replied. "Mmmm, it smells great in here; did you guys take out Indian food or something?"

"You mother made a wonderful curried soup. I just finished a bowl."

"Stay, Daddy, please. I want to tell you all about the swim meet," Sam crooned, her arms around her father's neck. When she stood so close to him it was obvious their colouring was identical. They even had the same cowlick on the left side of their foreheads, a cowlick that had made it impossible for Samantha ever to have bangs.

Liz felt her heart break a little more. She was surprised that any of it was still intact.

Adam kissed the top of his daughter's wet head. "I have to do something upstairs, sweetheart. I just got home from work. But come visit me in about an hour and I'll give you dessert, and we can talk. I bought some of that raspberry gelato you like."

"I'm trying not to eat junk food. But I'll come see you after I get my homework done. I have to finish an essay for English. And then I need to go over my notes for a bio test tomorrow."

"If you want, I can quiz you on the biology. Bye, Liz. Thanks for the soup."

"Bye, Adam."

Liz watched him walk out the door with more regret than she had for a long time. Clearly this time, with this particular girlfriend, it was serious. Her ego hadn't been resilient enough to stay married to a man who felt infidelity was just a tiny bit naughty, but as long as Adam's flings had stayed flings she'd held a special place in his life as the mother of his children. If he moved out to start a new life with Laura, that was sure to change. He might even have more children. Laura looked to be in her mid-twenties; it was likely she'd want to start her own family someday.

"Mummy?" Sammy was sitting at the kitchen table spooning up soup, her English text open before her.

"What is it, Sammy?"

She loved when her daughter called her "Mummy," though it rarely happened anymore. Adam had stayed "Daddy" however; maybe because he moved out when she was younger and she still spent less time with him than she did with Liz. Or perhaps all teenage girls liked their fathers better than they liked their mothers. Whatever the reason, it seemed to Liz that Adam was surrounded by adoring females these days.

"Do you think it's okay for me to say that Hamlet doesn't start out crazy but that by pretending that he is he kind of slips into insanity from time to time?"

Liz rapidly tried to collect her wandering thoughts. Her daughter still needed her, at least when it came to homework. *Hamlet.* A play she had studied in university a lifetime ago and seen only once onstage. Luckily, that had been just last year, a Soulpepper production right here in Toronto, so she still remembered it quite clearly. The prince in that interpretation of the play had been far from mad; he had been a sane man in an insane world, a world full of trickery, deceit, and evil.

"Doesn't he tell you that himself?"

"You mean when he says, 'I am but mad north-north-west: when the wind is southerly I know a hawk from a handsaw?'"

"Exactly."

"But isn't that just a fancy way of telling Rosencrantz and Guildenstern to bug off?"

"Sure, but he can be saying two things at the same time: warning them to leave him alone and also confessing that he doubts his own sanity. You don't have to choose just one meaning when it comes to Shakespeare, do you? He recognizes that life is complicated and contradictory. That's why his plays never go out of date."

"Good point, Mum. Thanks. I'm going to use that in my essay!" Sammy gave her a kiss and ran off to her room.

"That's not enough supper!" Liz shouted after her.

"I'm full," Sammy shouted back, leaving Liz to ponder her own words.

Life was not simple. It was full of contradictions. On the one hand, tonight Sammy had actually had some soup, kissed her, asked for her help; on the other hand, Liz hardly saw either of her children these days and they never seemed to eat together as a family. Adam recognized that they were growing up while she refused to. He was moving ahead with a new love but she was stuck in a rut, at the mercy of decisions made by other people.

He was right: she needed to start planning for the future.

Despite her overt resistance, she had already made a tentative stab at planning; Adam just didn't know it. Liz had not told him about James Scott's visit or his estimate of what the building was worth, which was considerably more than they had anticipated, because she hadn't been ready to put things in motion. She couldn't bear the thought of losing her safe haven.

She put a CD of Les Violons du Roy playing Piazzolla on the player and poured herself another glass of wine. Jasper stretched out along her legs, taking up at least as much space on the sofa as she did. *Sofa, chesterfield, davenport, couch, divan, settee*: she tried to calm her whirling thoughts by thinking of all the possible names for the piece of furniture she was lying on. Finding synonyms for things was a word game she often challenged herself with. Usually it absorbed her attention, but it wasn't working this evening because, deep down, she knew that Adam was right. She couldn't expect him to continue subsidizing her business if it was holding him back from what he wanted to do with his own life. And if what he wanted included playing what they used to call "chesterfield rugby" with a Brazilian hottie half his age, it was none of her goddamn business. Hmmm. Maybe that's where the name *loveseat* came from?

It wasn't surprising Adam had gone on the prowl for more attractive women, given what a scintillating wit she was. Still, Adam's trip abroad with Laura would give her time to get her act together. It would be fantastic if he came back to discover that Liz had come up with a solid plan to buy him out; if she could take control of the situation she wouldn't feel so helpless.

But how was she supposed to find a business partner? The bookstore wasn't profitable enough to support a second person. The only reason Georgia was willing to work part-time for low wages was that she was pursuing a doctorate in biochemistry and liked to give her overburdened synapses an occasional vacation.

Somebody with more money than brains might be interested in buying the building itself as an investment. It was weird the way everything, these days, brought her back to real estate. Actually, it was weird the way it was called "real" estate in the first place, as though all the other kinds of wealth were illusory. And "realty" sounded a lot like "reality," didn't it? Just put the "I" in — the ego, the person — like turning a building into a stage for human actions.

"MUM, ARE YOU OKAY?" her son's voice broke into her rambling thoughts.

"Yeah, sure," she replied, opening her eyes. "Why?"

"I thought you were having a migraine."

"No, I was just thinking. Do you want some dinner, Joshie?"

"Too late. I was so hungry after volleyball I bought a sub on the way home."

"There's only soup anyway."

"Me growing boy. Me need meat," Josh grunted, sticking out his jaw and swinging his arms in his best impersonation of a caveman.

"I know you do, sweetie, but meat grosses your sister out."

"That's another good reason to like it."

"When are you two going to start being nice to each other?"

"We are nice to each other. This is what nice looks like between brothers and sisters."

"I don't remember so much teasing between your uncle Michael and me."

"Because no one ever talked in your house. Remember?"

"Why do you always have to be so smart?"

"Good genes, Mum. Good genes," Josh said, pouring himself a glass of milk and grabbing a fistful of cookies. Liz stood up and rinsed her wineglass out in the sink. She'd brooded enough for one night.

"Put those on a plate, please. I don't want crumbs all over your room."

"Boy, are you ever grumpy tonight. Bad day at the Dog?"

"No, it was a good day. Georgia sold some books for once." Should she tell him about his father and Laura moving in together? About having to find a new partner or sell the bookstore? No, not yet; after all, it might never happen.

"Well, something's eating you, Mum. You can tell me. I am your oldest and wisest child."

"'Oldest' by all of ten minutes, and 'wisest' is debatable. But you're right, I am kind of preoccupied." She took a deep breath, aware of how silly what she was about to say would sound to her ever-skeptical son. "Remember that nice new neighbour I told you about? Max?"

"The retired prof?"

"Yes. Because I couldn't stop thinking about the body I found in the park, wondering what happened to him and why, Max is helping me do a little private investigating."

"Wow, watch out, bad guys! The new dynamic duo — Dead Language Guy and Library Lady — is hot on your trail."

"Scoff if you must, but it's making me feel better."

"Actually, it's kind of cool, Mum; I shouldn't have put you down. What kind of stuff are you doing?"

"Not much so far. We've searched the Net. And we interviewed a real estate agent from the dead man's firm, pretending Max wanted to buy a house in the neighbourhood."

"Did the agent have any inside dope?"

"Not really. She spent the whole time making goo-goo eyes at Max."

"Gross!"

"Oh right, I forgot. Old people have no sex drive. Except for your father, that is."

"What?" Josh looked up sharply.

"Never mind. Should I put this soup away or do you think you'll get hungry again later?"

"You can leave it out. I'll probably finish it off before bed. But don't think I didn't notice you changing the subject. You can't always distract me with food, Mum."

"Maybe not always. But you have to admit that it works most of the time. Here, take an apple to go with all those cookies. When you're around me you need to at least pretend to eat healthy."

THE SECURE youth custody centre wasn't exactly a prison and it wasn't exactly a school, but it was the first place in many years that he felt at home. For once he was with people just like him: abandoned boys, angry boys, sad, wary, and tired boys. Boys who had been largely neglected, except for those occasions when they were being abused. Boys who were expected to get into trouble and therefore shipped off to isolated places where there was no trouble for them to get into.

These boys weren't friends and they didn't form a new family, but they understood each other without needing to talk about what they'd been through. On the other hand, the counsellors at the centre were obsessed with talking, always urging them to "get in touch with their feelings." The counsellors insisted that "no one could go forward in life unless he came to terms with his past," and offered boxes of tissues followed by punching bags as cures for grief and rage. But among themselves the boys didn't waste words. Instead, they concentrated on getting strong. So strong that no one could ever hurt them again.

A lot of the boys lifted weights, partly for self-defence, partly because they were full of resentment and nervous energy and didn't know what else to do. The counsellors encouraged this activity, since exercise was "a healthy outlet" for "working through their issues." Although he had always been small for his age, and timid, he soon discovered he was stronger than he looked. When he had a growth spurt, things got easier, and he worked out more and more. He liked keeping too busy to think. He liked being so hungry at mealtimes that he could eat seconds of everything. He liked being so exhausted at the end of the day that he fell into a deep dreamless sleep the minute his head hit the pillow.

He especially liked his new muscles. When he arrived at the centre he was small and pale and silent and everyone had called him "Ghost," but now he found himself stealing glances at himself in the mirror, pleased with what he saw. He wasn't a skinny little creep anymore and despite the fact that he was blind without his glasses, none of the bullies picked on him. His crime, being unusually dramatic, had earned him that much respect. And soon he would be a man, and free. For the first time in his life he began to imagine that he might be able to make a life for himself; though not a sure thing, the future seemed a possibility.

7

Even the pretence of healthy eating was abandoned as Hallowe'en approached. Though Liz still shopped at the farmers' market, she spent more time sculpting rats and skulls out of marzipan than she did coming up with inventive uses for locally grown root vegetables. And she'd finally capitulated to Georgia and festooned the shop with orange and black streamers and slid a couple of black cats onto the mantel between the wooden dogs. She'd even splurged on a life-sized plastic skeleton to pose in a rocking chair in the window surrounded by the scariest books she had in stock: *Dracula, Frankenstein, The House with the Clock in its Walls, Coraline, The Haunting of Hill House, The Exorcist, The Shining, The Turn of the Screw, The Strange Case of Dr. Jekyll and Mr. Hyde,* and *The*

Complete Stories of Franz Kafka. For a joke, Georgia substituted books on financial management, weight control, and wedding planning, until Liz noticed and made her change them all back.

Still, when Outside of a Dog was quiet and she'd put in the minimal amount of bookkeeping required to keep it going, Liz tried to compile a record of any and all properties sold by James Scott. She thought an Internet search would be the likeliest route to find such information and thereby uncover potential candidates for a homicidal grudge, whether they were disappointed clients or rival agents. But all she could find online were properties for which Mr. Scott had been the listing agent prior to his death. When she finally conceded defeat and called the Real Estate Council of Ontario for advice, the brisk woman who answered the phone announced that the kind of information Liz was looking for was not available to members of the public. It was possible to find out past sales prices for properties by searching their titles, but there was no way to investigate the dealings of any individual agent unless there had been complaints, in which case a list of convictions dating back to 2003 could be found on the Council's website. Liz thanked the woman, feeling much less inadequate than she had prior to the phone call, and immediately clicked on the link suggested.

Unfortunately for her, there was no "James Scott" on the real estate blacklist. In fact, he was on precious few lists anywhere, except for a couple about industry award-winners. One of those included a photograph of him looking dashing in a perfectly tailored tuxedo. Liz suddenly realized that she didn't know any men who owned tuxedos. A few male friends and relations had rented penguin suits for proms or weddings, but none of them had ever looked as good as James Scott did in his designer duds. He really had been an extremely handsome man. That she found herself attracted to him despite the fact that he was dead and suspecting that he had probably been involved in some shady business, was clearly evidence that she needed more romance in her life.

Correction: not more romance. Any romance at all would be an improvement. In the five years since Adam moved out, she'd slept with precisely two men: an old university friend passing through town on business who invited her to join him for a drink at his hotel and got to see a lot more of her in the next few days than either of them had anticipated, and the recently divorced and incorrigibly morose father of one of Sam's friends, whom she comforted for a few months and then spent the rest of the year avoiding at parent-teacher interviews and school concerts. She had yet to bring anyone back to the flat although she had gone on a couple of other dates. Somehow, despite the conveyor belt of females upstairs at Adam's place, Liz felt uncomfortable dating in front of her kids. Periodically one of them might make a joke about needing to find her a boyfriend but she didn't think they meant it. And to be honest, she wasn't particularly lonely. But the allure of James Scott suggested that she was finally finding men attractive again, and surely that was a good thing.

There was another beautiful picture of the guy on the company website, from whence he dispensed advice about how to prepare a house for sale (remove clutter, pack up personal memorabilia, buy flowers, put fresh towels in the bathroom, bake cookies or boil cinnamon sticks on the stove to create a welcoming aroma), and observed that the opening of a Starbucks franchise was a good indicator that a neighbourhood was becoming gentrified. Such platitudes would surely have earned him the sobriquet of "Captain Obvious" from Josh. They revealed nothing about their speaker except that, like most of those who do well in business, he told his clients exactly what they expected to hear. All she could find out about the murder victim was that he was handsome and successful; the latter she had known since the police rifled his pockets and found his car keys and the former, although it made her investigation more tantalizing, hardly seemed relevant.

While Liz pursued her solitary research, Max continued with the fieldwork. He agreed to visit a couple more real estate agents on his own after Liz convinced him that her inability to keep a straight face when he got into his routine was bound to make people suspicious. He had actually succeeded in getting a nervous fellow with a painful-looking boil on his neck to declare that there was "something fishy about James Scott," and that when he'd heard a real estate agent had been murdered he'd known at once who it would be. But whether because Max's subsequent questions were overly probing or because his informant genuinely had zilch with which to back up his suspicions, that was all he got. Ultimately, the man confessed that he knew nothing incriminating about Mr. Scott; that his had been an instinctive kind of dislike, and probably an unworthy one. Furthermore, he was so embarrassed by his outburst against the defenceless dead man that Max felt compelled to change the topic of their conversation to the ever-reliable comparison of Montreal's merits versus those of Toronto, a topic that engaged them for a good twenty minutes and resulted in a list of recommended eating establishments, which he flourished at Liz as the only tangible evidence of his inquiries.

"Seneca once said that it is better to know useless things than to know nothing, but I'm not sure I agree with him."

"This list of restaurants isn't useless," Liz replied. "Just expensive. Appetizers for twenty dollars? Main courses for thirty-five dollars? These places are way out of my league; I'm more the 'let's-split-a-$6.95-lunch-special-with-an-extra-spring-roll' kind of girl."

"I hate splitting my food with anyone."

"That must be why you bought all these individual pastries, which are exquisite but so expensive, rather than a whole cake."

They were having tea in Max's dining room. Even though there were only the two of them, a damask cloth covered the table, which was set with pale blue Wedgwood china and an exquisite Georgian silver tea service. As Liz dropped individual Demerara sugar cubes into her cup with a pair of tiny silver tongs, she couldn't help thinking how much her mother would admire this man. Everything about Max, from his tan cashmere sweater to the thick oriental carpets on his floor, the warm smell of almond oil that came from his recently polished mahogany furniture, and the fresh bouquet of peach-coloured roses on his enormous leather-topped desk, suited Mrs. Ryerson's idea of civilized living. Each object in Max's apartment was carefully chosen and well maintained; elegant but not flashy; calculated to give pleasure. He lived alone and had no one to please but himself. He didn't have to worry about skate blades nicking his floor or muddy paw prints on his sofa or the daily indignities family life imposes on any space, no matter how carefully appointed.

Not that Liz's own home was carefully appointed. She had no one from whom to inherit antiques and no money to buy them. Most of her stuff had come not from an ancestor or an auction house but from IKEA, that temple of plausible style and flimsy mass-production, a place the door of which she suspected Professor Maxime Bertrand had never darkened. She could not imagine him sitting on the floor struggling with impenetrable instructions and an Allen key.

"You're probably right," he was saying. "The thought of buying a cake unnerves me. What if I can't divide it up evenly? Will I still get my fair share? Or even worse, what if we don't eat it all and it goes to waste? Well, the whole enterprise seems impossibly complicated."

"Clearly you grew up in a big family with a limited budget."

"Indeed. My parents were Québécois *pur laines*. They had ten children. Clever deduction, Detective Ryerson."

"I wish I were as clever at solving our real-life murder mystery," Liz sighed. "I'm ready to give up this detecting gig, Max. It's a waste of time. Even the Real Estate Council has nothing about James Scott on file anywhere. They only keep track of people they've had to discipline for professional misconduct. Unfortunately for us, he wasn't one of those."

"So maybe this crime has nothing to do with his work."

"Do you think maybe he was a random victim?"

"No, I don't," Max said thoughtfully. "He was hit over the head hard enough to kill him; that's hardly what anyone would call random. He was either lured to an isolated place or dumped there. Either way, the evidence suggests that somebody planned his death."

COURTESY OF GLOBAL WARMING, Hallowe'en was balmier than usual. When her own children were younger, Liz had spent many hours sewing elaborate costumes to fit over their snowsuits, but this year girls frolicked in sparkly princess gowns, and boys zoomed around as superheroes. Nobody had to worry about the full glory of their masquerade being obscured by winter coats. She herself was happy to spend All Hallow's Eve curled up in a rocking chair with a big bowl of Kraft caramels and Hershey's Kisses in her lap. She'd always had a sweet tooth; this annual sugar frenzy merely gave her licence to succumb to it without guilt. And the twins shared her enthusiasm for sweets, though they preferred commercial confectionary to her homemade experiments. In fact, they compensated for being too old to go trick-or-treating by stretching the single canonical night of dressing up and eating too much candy into two solid weeks of partying.

Or they had done, until this year. For some reason, Sammy had recently decided that candy was "toxic" and refused to eat it — as well as a lot of other things like cheese and ice cream and baked goods and pasta — anymore. She'd always had a swimmer's build, sleek and toned, but tonight, in a skin-tight black-cat outfit, she looked almost gaunt.

"At least have a glass of milk or something before you go out," Liz begged. "Or how about if I make you a smoothie? This banana is perfectly ripe and there are some organic blueberries in the freezer. I could put in some yogurt or some hemp seed for protein."

"We're going to a party, Mother. There's going to be lots of food there. Will you please stop nagging me to eat all the time?"

"Don't worry, Ms. Ryerson. I'll make sure this kitten gets some kibble," said Derek, the new friend Samantha had finally introduced to the family. He was dressed as a vampire, a costume that suited his high cheekbones, dark eyes, and scarlet lips. Liz found it more than a little disquieting, because the boy had such white teeth and smiled so often.

She couldn't help wondering if Sammy's surliness and rejection of food had anything to do with her relationship with Derek, whom she seemed to idolize. For weeks before they'd actually met the boy, they'd heard stories about what Derek did, and what Derek said; how he was amazing on guitar and had a thousand hits on YouTube. How he was auditioning for movies all the time and still kept up brilliantly in school. That he looked like a movie star. Liz never would have predicted that her spunky daughter could be made insecure by anybody, but Sammy was a teenager now, and apparently unable to sail through adolescence with the easy confidence she had as a child.

In retrospect, being a parent had been easier when the kids were younger. Emotionally easier, that is; there had been more heavy lifting but a lot less angst. Liz looked at the bowl of candy in her lap. If more trick-or-treaters didn't show up soon, she would have to eat the whole thing herself. The neighbourhood kids knew she would wait for them at the bookstore but even so, she didn't have many visitors, being on a commercial strip. Most parents took their children to tour the residential streets, which were brightly lit and extravagantly decorated. Even the grownups in Hillcrest Village were devoted to Hallowe'en, some dressing up as witches and pirates to accompany their offspring door-to-door, others transforming their homes into haunted houses complete with special effects like flying bats and ghouls jumping out of coffins. Liz had decided not to wear a costume this year, but Jasper sat proudly beside her in a white button-down shirt accessorized by a red clip-on bow tie, his long front legs poking through the shirt sleeves and his tail swishing freely out the back.

She had finally run out of candy and gone up to her flat when a crash from below triggered the burglar alarm. Jasper immediately started barking and scratching at the door, adding to the frenzy. Liz pushed him away and then reconsidered. If there were intruders, she might be very glad to have a dog with her, even Jasper, who never looked particularly threatening and looked even less so than usual in tonight's get-up. She quickly stripped him of shirt and bow tie, her heart pounding almost as loudly as the alarm. Should she go downstairs and turn it off? But maybe there was a robber down there. Where was Adam, and why couldn't he hear the racket? He must be out partying with people half his age.

The phone screeched, startling her. It was not Adam but the alarm company.

"May I please speak to Ms. Ryerson?"

"You're speaking to her."

"Are you aware the glass break detector has been triggered at Outside of a Dog Bookstore on St. Clair Avenue West?" the annoyingly composed female voice continued.

"Of course I'm aware! You can probably hear the alarm in the background right now if you listen."

"Do you want us to send a security guard over to check it out?"

"Why can't you send the police?"

"They'll charge you a hundred dollars if they have to go out for a false alarm, Miss."

"This is not a false alarm," Liz said indignantly. "I was sitting right here and I heard a big crash."

"Well, if you authorize a police call, I can make one."

"Yes, please. Tell them to ring my doorbell after they've checked the place. I'll stay upstairs in my flat and wait."

But she couldn't wait. Even though she was frightened, she tiptoed down the stairs to the street with Jasper on a short leash beside her, wondering if she would be able to discover what was going on without endangering herself. She lurked in the dark doorway for a few minutes, resisting the dog's attempts to pull her outside. She could see a cluster of teenagers waiting at the bus stop and an innocuous-looking couple in matching beige trenchcoats walking home arm-in-arm. She took a deep breath and slid out of the shadows. It was immediately clear what the problem was.

"Oh, no," Liz howled. "Why would anybody do this?"

Someone, somehow, had broken her front window. It was webbed with cracks and at the site of impact there was a jagged hole like the mouth of a jack-o'-lantern. The front door was still locked, however, so it didn't appear that anyone had actually entered the store.

She unlocked the door with unaccustomed difficulty. Her hands were shaking as she turned off the alarm. Her emotions vacillated between rage at the exterior damage and relief that the interior seemed unscathed. To make sure that nobody sinister was still lurking, she switched on all the lights and shouted, "Get the hell out of my shop, you bastard!"

Jasper started barking at the anger in her voice. Nobody appeared. Liz walked down one side of the store to her desk, scrutinized it and its contents, continued through the back rooms, and then returned along the other side and back to the front door. As far as she could tell, nothing had been taken. The till wasn't forced, her computer and printer were still on the table, the kitchen appliances and CD player were where they belonged, and the storeroom was untouched. Darwin the tortoise looked somewhat stressed out, his leathery neck pulled all the way into his shell and his eyes blinking faster than usual, but except for a pile of broken glass below the window itself, everything seemed to be fine. Liz went back outside to wait for the police, hoping that she'd simply been the victim of a Hallowe'en prank.

"Poor Lizzie. What a mess." It was Marcia, the lady who lived over the flower shop next door. She crushed Liz to her generous, cinnamon-coloured bosom. "Why couldn't they just smash a pumpkin in front of your door or throw some eggs at it?"

"I guess those kinds of pranks are too old-fashioned," said Liz, very glad Marcia had joined her. It was hard to be scared with Marcia radiating righteous indignation beside her.

"Was anything stolen?"

"Probably not. I didn't check all that thoroughly, but nothing inside was disturbed and the front door was still locked."

"Well, here comes a police car. They're a lot quicker than usual. When the corner store was robbed last Hallowe'en it took the cops at least an hour to get here. Mr. Kim was so angry that he accused them of being racist."

"Yeah, I remember. I was so surprised, because I'd never even heard him raise his voice before. That man is the soul of politeness." She sighed.

"Do you want me to stay with you for moral support?"

"No, it's okay, really. Unless you have any idea who could have done this."

"I wish I could help, but I didn't see a thing."

"Hey, I know you," said the policeman squeezing his bulk out from behind the wheel.

"Officer MacDonald. From Wychwood Park."

"Right you are."

"We've got to stop meeting like this," Liz said wryly. "At least there's no dead body this time. Just a broken window."

"It's not the only one tonight. The exact same thing happened on College Street an hour ago," he said, pulling out a notepad and a ballpoint pen that looked like it would break in his meaty paw. "Was anything taken?"

"Not that I can tell. Was the business on College another bookstore?"

"Nope, a hair salon. Real thieves target jewellers or electronics stores, so this is probably just a bunch of teenagers driving around looking for trouble. I assume you're insured?"

"Of course she is," Marcia interrupted indignantly. "Now, go ahead and write up your report. The poor woman doesn't want to stay up all night while you dilly-dally."

"Thanks, Marcia," Liz said. "I'm sure Officer MacDonald will perform his duties with the utmost dispatch."

"I'll go then," said Marcia, giving the policeman a last suspicious look. "But you'd better be good to Ms. Ryerson, you hear?"

"Yes, ma'am," Officer MacDonald said, saluting Marcia as she marched off. Liz laughed. Sometimes she wished she had just one ounce of her neighbour's self-assurance.

"Here's the procedure. Just like your friend said, I write up a report. Then you call the twenty-four-hour window-replacement people. You'll have to pay them up front, but then you send in the claim with my report and your insurance company will pay you back, minus the deductible. It's totally routine."

"Not for me. But this seems to be my month for experiencing all kinds of crimes for the first time."

"I'm sorry. This must be hard for you," said MacDonald, unexpectedly. The phrase sounded a bit stilted; Liz couldn't help wondering whether he'd been forced to undergo sensitivity training since their last encounter.

"Can you tell me if you've made any progress with the other case?"

"I'm afraid not."

"But I was the one who found the body, and I can't stop thinking about it. I can't even sleep anymore."

Her voice was getting shrill. She was ashamed of being histrionic, but at the same time she recognized that appearing helpless and feminine would probably appeal to Officer

MacDonald, who seemed like an old-fashioned kind of fellow. Besides, she was entitled to indulge her inner damsel-in-distress once in a while. She really did feel vulnerable, and threatened, and was utterly weary of trying to manage everything by herself. Liz gave in to her tears, and right on cue Jasper started whining and licking her hand. *Good boy*, she thought. *Between the two of us we will wear this guy down in no time.*

"I can see how upset you are, ma'am, and to tell you the truth, I was pretty shaken up myself. But ever since that homicide detective told me off last time for talking too much, I've been keeping my lip zipped."

"Why? This is your beat, not his, right? So you should be the one to decide what the local residents need to know." She could see him hesitating and was amazed to recognize that she was manipulating him like a pro. Marcia would have been proud of her.

"I don't know that much, honestly."

"Then there's no reason to feel guilty for giving me an update." Liz stood her ground, meeting the policeman eye to eye.

MacDonald blinked first. "This is just between us, okay?"

Liz just nodded: a useful tactic she had learned from her kids for avoiding incriminating answers. If she didn't actually say anything, she wouldn't feel like such a liar when she inevitably passed the information on to Max.

"Well, the victim had no record, and his condo was clean: no drugs, no pornography, nothing incriminating, not even an unpaid parking ticket. And he wasn't robbed, even though he had a lot of dough on him as well as a nice watch, a cellphone, and a laptop."

"Sorry, but I don't understand the significance of all this."

"The point I'm trying to make is that this murder wasn't about money or gangs or anything else. It was personal. There's no reason for you to worry. His death doesn't mean there will be more violence in your neighbourhood."

"But why did it happen here in the first place?"

He took a deep breath and then paused, as if uncertain whether or not to proceed. She waited for a beat and then, when he said nothing, she repeated slowly and emphatically, "If only James Scott was the target, and he wasn't even local, why did the murder happen here?"

"It's possible that it didn't happen here. The scene-of-the-crime officers found a trail of broken vegetation showing that the body had been dragged down the hill to where we found it. Probably the perp intended to throw it into the pond and didn't realize that there was a fence in the way, because it was already dark by the time the murder took place and besides, everything was so overgrown."

"That makes sense," Liz nodded. She'd tried to get through the fence herself once or twice to have better access to bird-watching around the pond, but the gate had always been locked. "Last question. I promise. Do you guys have any idea who committed the crime?"

"Not yet, but we're working on it. Apparently Mr. Scott got a call at the real estate office right before he disappeared. Scott was out, so the secretary gave the caller his cellphone number to try instead. When we traced both calls, they led back to a public telephone box on Yonge Street, so that was no help. Our best clue so far is some tire tracks from a truck that didn't belong to a resident of Wychwood Park, or to anyone else who normally works in the area."

"I guess that's good news for me, since it means the murderer probably wasn't local," said Liz slowly, pondering the meaning of what she had just heard. She shivered, then realized that she had been shivering for some time. She'd run outside without a coat, and the cold was exacerbated by her nerves.

"Exactly. So like I said, you're safe. Sorry you had to be the victim of another crime so soon, but this vandalism was just bad luck."

"Hopefully."

"The official police document will be ready in a day or two. Here's the number to call to check if it's ready. You can come pick it up yourself, or have Division fax it directly to your insurance company, okay?"

"Okay, thanks. Any suggestions about who I should call to fix the window?"

"There's a bunch of twenty-four-hour places in the phone book. They're all pretty much the same. They'll come and measure the window; if it's a standard size they might be able to replace it right away. Otherwise they'll board it up so no one can get in and then come back tomorrow with the new glass."

"That would be great."

"And please, don't repeat the stuff I told you about the case. I don't need any more headaches."

"Don't worry, Officer MacDonald. You can trust me. And thank you so much. I feel like you've given me my life back."

8

B Y THE TIME THE kids got home from their party, the shop window was boarded up. Liz was wearing her coziest pyjamas and had exchanged the wooden salad bowl full of Hallowe'en candy for a couple of inches of Glenfiddich in her only Waterford crystal tumbler. She'd bought the bottle on the way home from her last trip to the UK, at the enormous duty-free store at Heathrow where they gave out enough free samples to make everything in sight seem like a good bargain. The bottle of scotch had been sitting in her cupboard for two years, memorializing a passing delusion about her tastes and habits. Now was obviously the perfect time to open it.

She was watching an insipid talk show on which a skeletal starlet with lips like a carp was pitching her latest movie when

Josh and Sammy pounded up the stairs. Josh reached the top first, shouting before he even reached her, "Mum, what happened to the store?"

"Are you okay?" Sammy added.

"Oh my God, she's drinking scotch. Mum never drinks scotch!"

"Someone broke the window, that's all; everything's fine. And this isn't just any old scotch: it's twelve-year-old single malt whiskey, aged in the misty Highlands, flown over the Atlantic Ocean in my carry-on luggage with the sherbet lemons, Marks & Spencer knickers, and PG Tips tea bags."

"But you're drinking it," Josh insisted.

"No shit, Sherlock."

"And you're swearing," Sammy added.

"Did you guys think you invented drinking and swearing?" Liz asked sweetly.

"No, but Mummy ..." Sammy started.

"And we weren't drinking much tonight, just beer," Josh added.

"Glad to hear it. That's one less thing to worry about," Liz replied.

"Where's Daddy?"

"Gallivanting around with Miss Brazil."

"Were you all alone when the window got smashed?"

"No. Jasper was by my side, faithful as always. At least I can count on the dog for loyal companionship."

"I'm sorry you were by yourself. I'm sure you were scared." Sammy gave her a big hug for the first time in weeks. Hugging her back, Liz was shocked at how prominent her ribs were.

She looked up at Josh over Sammy's head and squeezed the air behind her daughter's back to indicate how narrow her body had become. Josh nodded. He was worried too.

"Thank you, my sweet girl. I needed that. But really, everything's fine. Nothing else was damaged, and the window will be replaced tomorrow. And my business insurance will cover everything but the two-hundred-dollar deductible. So let's talk about something else, all right? How was your party?"

"Hot. I think I drank three whole bottles of water."

"That's all you had, Sam. I was watching you and the Count," Josh interjected.

"Will you please stop calling Derek 'the Count'? It's not funny anymore. And why is everyone obsessing over what I eat?"

"Because we love you, and we're worried about you," Liz said. "Sammy, you're getting too thin."

"You never say Josh is too thin."

"Because I eat like a pig," Josh pointed out.

"Your brother is right. If you were eating properly, I wouldn't be concerned about your weight either."

"I'm just not hungry these days. Probably because I've finally stopped growing. You should be glad, Mum. You won't have to keep buying me new clothes all the time."

"Are you anxious about something?" Liz asked, refusing to be derailed.

"No, everything's great."

"Well, I'm making you a doctor's appointment in the morning."

"You're the one who needs to go to the doctor. You've been

a wreck ever since you found that body in the park. And you're taking it out on me!"

Sammy ran into her bedroom and slammed the door. Josh sat down on the sofa next to his mother with a sigh.

"Well, that went rather well, I must say," he said in a fake English accent. And then, in his own aggrieved voice, "Mum, I can't believe there aren't any Hershey's Kisses left."

"What's going on with Sammy? Do you have any idea?"

"Yeah. Its name is Derek and he's a bad influence. How about the caramels? Did you eat all of those too?"

"I had a lot of trick-or-treaters. It wasn't just me," Liz protested. "Don't change the subject. Why don't you like Derek?"

"Because he's a bullshit artist. And Sammy not eating? I think it started because Derek was waving around a magazine with photos of him surrounded by size-zero models, so now she's worried he'll dump her for someone thinner."

"Derek's a model? I thought Sammy said he was a musician and an actor."

"He's trying to be an actor, but meanwhile he's doing fashion shoots. It's perfect for him. The guy's all surface. Sammy's way too good for him."

"Have you told her that?"

"She just says I'm jealous because I don't have a girl-friend. Frankly, I don't need the abuse."

"Oh, dear. Sounds just like your father's response when I asked whether he might be rushing into things with Lah-oh-ra."

"Fools in love, Mum. They're just fools in love. Now budge over. There's an all-night horror-movie marathon on TV that will take your mind off your worries. This one's a classic."

"*Attack of the Killer Tomatoes*? Wow, I didn't realize that was a real movie. I always thought it was just the punchline to a bad joke."

"You gotta see it to believe it."

"The way my life is going these days, Joshie, I find the idea of man-eating vegetables less frightening than people breaking into my bookstore. There's no way I'm going to be able to sleep tonight, so I may as well stay up and watch the movie with you."

THE NEXT MORNING THE window was repaired and everything appeared normal, but Liz still found herself too wound up to work. When Georgia showed up for her Wednesday afternoon gig, Liz planted herself in front of the computer and read up on anorexia nervosa, growing more and more agitated by the minute.

Sammy had some symptoms of the disease such as weight loss, irritability, secretiveness, refusal to eat meals with the family, food aversions, and obsessive exercising. The last of these was nothing new, since she'd always loved sports, and weren't all teenagers irritable and secretive at times? But she lacked the most dramatic ones, including swollen joints, acne, bad breath, hair loss, and cold intolerance, as well as others with complex medical names and even more dire consequences. Meanwhile, every website she consulted said that the worst thing a concerned parent could do was to nag a teenage girl about her poor eating habits, which was exactly what Liz had been doing. But who else would see Sammy often enough, or care enough, to monitor what she was eating?

Frustrated, Liz called the family doctor and was put on hold, then disconnected. She called four more times, each time receiving a busy signal. No, she did not want Bell to notify her when the line became available; she wanted to speak to some-body *right now*. She even considered going to the office in person, but thought better of it. That was precisely the kind of behaviour that would make it seem like she was the one with the problem rather than Sammy.

Unable to settle down to any other kind of activity, Liz prowled around the store, flipping through child-rearing guides and health manuals, the kinds of books she generally avoided. Inter-estingly, there was not much about anorexia in Dr. Spock. Although the disease had first been identified in the nineteenth century, nowadays it was affecting younger and younger people, probably as a consequence of their bombardment by glamorous imagery of wraiths whose frail bodies did not interrupt the line of their clothes. In fact, the age of onset had fallen from thirteen to nine, in sync with the fashion industry's use of younger and younger models. Ten times more girls succumbed to the malady than boys.

Yadda, yadda, yadda, as Josh would have said. She couldn't believe that she was reading this stuff, partly because the psy-chology involved seemed glib and superficial and partly because it seemed to have so little to do with her own daughter, who had never been neurotic, or suffered from low self-esteem, or been a slave to fashion, or had any of the other issues suggested as predictors of susceptibility to anorexia. Perhaps perfectionism; Sammy definitely was a bit of a perfectionist.

On the other hand, there was an interesting link between

anorexia and migraines, and Liz herself suffered from migraines. Some people suggested loss of appetite could result from a zinc deficiency or insufficient intake of omega-3 fatty acids and since Sammy was a vegetarian, maybe there were things missing in her diet. Liz had been concerned for a long time that she didn't get enough protein. They should go down to that nice Korean place for tofu soup; Sammy loved that soup as well as the little dishes of sweet soybeans that came with it. She'd get a good dose of protein that way. They would go this weekend, for sure.

She put Darwin the tortoise on her desk for moral support before calling the doctor again, and got through, just as the office was closing. He agreed to see Samantha after school on Friday. He also noted that while Liz's concern was reasonable, jumping to the conclusion that Sammy had a full-blown eating disorder was not. Although most teenage girls put on weight when they stopped growing, others slimmed down, he said. Did Liz remember what her own weight had been like at that age?

She had been pretty skinny, she admitted.

Well, then, he said. Try not to worry too much.

Liz hung up the telephone feeling remarkably dissatisfied. The websites told her not to nag, the doctor told her not to worry, and now she had to wait. Was there no area in her life where she was in control?

"Can you hold the fort, Georgia? And the tortoise? I'm taking Jasper for a walk," she said. Ignoring her own empty stomach, she headed over to Wychwood Park for the first time since she had discovered the body of James Scott.

The streets were full of adults heading home from work and a few loitering kids still on a sugar high from the previous night's festivities. Usually she took the dog out at quieter times of day when they didn't have to negotiate so much foot traffic or worry about impatient drivers running red lights. There were several other dog-walkers about, enjoying the mild weather before dinner. Once they reached the confines of Wychwood Park, almost the only people they saw were those at the end of a leash or pushing baby buggies. Jasper insisted on greeting each and every one of them.

It was a good thing, in a way, because it made the place seem less sinister. Dogs and babies had that in common: their cheerfulness always made it seem that life was good and the world was a friendly place even when this was manifestly not the case. She knew very well that things *were* good for her, a middle-class lady running a bookstore in a wealthy city, away from war and pestilence and earthquakes, et cetera et cetera. How lucky she was to be worried about whether her beautiful daughter was eating as much as she should rather than if she could afford to feed her at all! Liz didn't want to be a self-absorbed whiner, but sometimes it was difficult to tell what was a legitimate concern and what was an overreaction, especially when it came to her children.

Without realizing it, she had automatically stopped at the eastern edge of the pond where Jasper usually positioned himself to bark at the ducks. The birds were still lazily swimming around the pond pecking at the floating scum, either bereft of the normal instinct to fly south or ignoring it in response to the uncharacteristically warm weather. Jasper told the birds exactly how contemptible he thought they were but they didn't respond to his furious barking. The familiar ritual having been enacted to everyone's satisfaction, Liz said, "Come on, boy," and they resumed walking.

"Your dog really hates those ducks, doesn't he?" remarked a woman with a beautiful Gordon setter, falling into step beside them. "Byron feels that way that about squirrels."

"Jasper isn't fond of squirrels either," Liz acknowledged. "But it's all an act. He would never attack them; he just likes to look tough."

"That's a good thing, isn't it? I want my dog to look tough because it makes me feel like no one will bother me when I'm walking him after dark."

"I guess so," said Liz. "But this isn't really a dangerous neighbourhood."

"I agree. Unfortunately that murder last month made people worry that property values here were going to plummet."

"You sound like a real estate agent."

"Probably because I'm studying to be one," the woman laughed. "I got burnt out after fifteen years as a nurse and decided to go into something completely different."

"Is it hard?"

"Not compared to night shift in the ICU. And at least in this job no one will throw a bedpan at me or spray me with HIV positive blood."

"I should hope not."

"Still, there are other problems. I had to buy a lot of nice clothes because I don't wear a uniform anymore and now I'm worried that I'm going through my savings too fast because even when I finally get to sell a house I won't get paid for months, until after the closing. I guess that's why so many people go into real estate as a second career."

"I'll keep that in mind if things don't work out with my bookstore," Liz said. Her mind was whirling. If real estate was traditionally a second career, she needed to find out what James Scott had been doing before he went into it.

"I ALREADY KNOW WHAT he was doing before," said Max. "Construction."

Liz had called him on the phone as soon as she got back, convinced he should stop his real estate investigation and find out what Scott had been up to in his earlier life.

"I got that information from La Belle Madame Horvath, while checking out a cozy duplex with original gumwood trim, stained glass, and an orange shag carpet that smelled like cat pee. It didn't seem important at the time."

"So he went from building houses into selling them."

"Apparently."

"Did Horvath happen to mention the name of the company he worked for?"

"No, I don't think so. Anyhow, you said you wanted to stop detecting, Liz. What made you change your mind?"

"I need the distraction, Max. I'm a nervous wreck right now. Josh is gearing up for the battle of the bands at his high school, so he's always over at the drummer's house practising and I hardly ever see him. Sammy's obsessed with her creepy new boyfriend and doesn't want to be with me either. And there are only so many walks a day I can take with poor old Jasper."

"Why is Sammy's boyfriend creepy?'

"He compliments me too often, and offers to help too much, and drops too many boastful comments about his accomplishments. And it's like he's cast a spell over Sammy. She walks around in a complete daze all the time."

"Well, Aristotle said that the young are permanently in a state resembling intoxication."

"Aristotle didn't know Samantha Silver. Until she met this boy Derek, she was the most focused kid around. Always clear about where she was going, what she was doing, and what she expected of other people. And not only that: she used to be very open with me. And with Adam too. She adores her dad and always talks to him. But she won't talk to either of us anymore."

"Does she confide in Josh?"

"No, because he made it clear that he doesn't trust Derek. He's been calling him 'the Count' since the boy dressed up as a vampire at Hallowe'en. It drives Sammy crazy."

"Hmm."

"It's terrible, Max. Sammy hardly ever eats with us any-more. In fact, I don't know what or when she's eating. It worries me sick. I'm taking her to the doctor next week for a checkup. She's angry about that too."

"What does Adam think?"

"All Adam can think about is this big trip he's going on with his girlfriend, 'Lah-oh-ra.' He's busy buying those hideous zip-off pants with hidden pockets that only Canadian tourists wear, and getting vaccinations, and chatting on the Internet with Australian potheads about the best beaches in Thailand.

SAFE AS HOUSES 109

And now that Lah-oh-ra's moved in upstairs, I can never get him alone for a private conversation."

"From the way you pronounce her name, I assume that Adam's girlfriend is Hispanic?"

"Brazilian, as it happens."

"And that you don't like her."

"I barely know her. I'm just a jealous old hag, that's all. She's much younger than me and has a body to die for and I'm the discarded first wife. The sloughed-off skin. A dead parrot."

"Not dead, just pining for the fjords," Max said, recognizing the allusion to the old Monty Python routine. Liz started laughing and then, abruptly, she was crying.

"Oh, I'm sorry, Max. You must think I'm such a cheap stereotype."

"Never, Liz. *Il n'y en a pas deux comme toi.*"

"You're so sweet. But I feel totally helpless right now. Especially because I don't know what to do about Sammy. Normally Adam would be the overprotective parent, not me, but he's going away for three whole months and it's made me realize how much I still count on him to help with the kids. And on top of that, he's determined to sell his share in the building when he comes back so that he can get a bigger place with Laura. I feel like I'm losing control of everything."

She sighed. "This is going to sound crazy, but I knew right away that finding that body was an evil omen. Every single day since then something else has gone wrong."

"Try to focus on one problem at a time. The most important thing right now is Sammy not eating properly. You have to talk to Adam about her before he leaves on his trip."

"I know, I know. Except that since he's head over heels himself, he won't see the problem, will he?"

"He might surprise you. Men can be pretty fierce when it comes to protecting their families. Even though Chantal's grown up now and lives so far away, I would hunt down and kill anyone who tried to harm her."

DESPITE HIS exemplary behaviour and the psychiatrist's opinion that he was unlikely to reoffend, he refused to ask for early release at the annual custody review. It wasn't just that he was comfortable at the centre; there was nowhere else for him to go. His mother had drunk herself to death not long after he was imprisoned and he'd had his fill of foster homes. Given the situation, the authorities agreed to let him stay where he was until he finished high school, by which time he had served the maximum sentence for second-degree murder.

The minute the authorities made him leave, he boarded a Greyhound bus travelling south to Toronto, where some of the older boys had already found jobs in the booming construction industry. Under the Young Offenders Act, they had been released from custody with no supervision and no support in making the transition back to society but, despite the squawking of well-intentioned social workers and childcare specialists, this was just fine with them. The last thing these boys wanted was someone in authority scrutinizing their actions. After all, they were now — for the first time in their short unhappy lives — masters of their own fates. And they were determined that nobody else was going to tell them what to do ever again.

The fact that they had committed serious crimes was irrelevant. Nobody cared what they'd done in the past as long as they showed up on time for their jobs and worked hard. To perform unskilled casual labour they didn't need references and, unlike other employers, their bosses didn't request a police record check. To work in construction, they didn't even need high school transcripts — though his were excellent, had anyone thought to ask.

But no one did ask. Nobody was interested in him, although he was interested in everything. Unlike the other guys at work, whose favourite activities were getting drunk and chasing girls, he spent his spare time training at the gym or reading at the library. He still didn't feel safe; he needed to become stronger and smarter, always stronger and smarter. Then maybe, one day, he could relax a little.

His vigilance was constant. He kept looking for clues about how other people — ordinary people — lived. Ever since he was a little boy, he had tried to please adults by reading their body language and anticipating their wishes. Back then, he did it to avoid being punished. Now he did it so he could fit in. He observed that in the big city people dressed nicely and walked quickly; they carried briefcases or backpacks and read newspapers or books on the subway; they didn't talk a lot because they all had somewhere to go.

Toronto was a very busy place, unlike the northern mill towns he was used to: towns people left and never returned to, towns in which buildings that wore out were never replaced. Everywhere he looked here old structures were being torn down and new ones were going up. And the people selling the new properties were making a lot more money than the poor jerks like him who were building them. He promised himself that someday he would be one of those other guys: a guy in a suit going home to a high-rise instead of a guy in a hard hat burrowing into a basement apartment with damp cement floors and no view. Someday he would be able to pour himself a glass of imported wine after work while soaking in a Jacuzzi. Someday he would stop looking over his shoulder and start enjoying his life.

With this ambition in mind, he worked hard and saved his money. He took books out of the library and read them on the subway. He didn't waste a minute of the five years it took for his juvenile records to be permanently sealed; he was always becoming, never just being. When the five years were up, he enrolled in a real estate course.

To his relief, in real estate — just like in construction — nobody cared what he'd done in the past as long as he showed up on time and worked hard. He'd already started wearing contact lenses because they were safer than glasses for someone working with heavy equipment; he had the lenses tinted a darker blue than his own eyes because he'd noticed how much their paleness unnerved people. Now, as a final break with the past, to exorcise the boy once known as "Ghost," he dyed his blond hair black. Best of all, he found a second-hand car in excellent condition and polished it patiently to a new-car shine. Real estate agents lived in their cars, he'd been told; an agent's car should be an extension of himself. Where his car came from — whether it had run over a pedestrian, or raced above the legal limit on poorly lit country roads, or just sat neglected for years in some little old lady's garage — no one would ever know. Just like him it was starting over; just like him, it was almost as good as new.

It was the year 2000. The new millennium. Anything was possible.

9

O N THURSDAY, AFTER SHE closed the shop and took Jasper for a walk, Liz forced herself to go upstairs and knock on Adam's door. He wasn't home, but Laura welcomed her in. She was dressed in a soft lilac cowl-neck sweater and jeans, her hair loosed from its usual severe ponytail, wearing no makeup or jewellery, not even her nose-stud. Like Laura herself, the place looked different than Liz remembered: softer and more welcoming. Apparently they had redecorated, or maybe it was the addition of some of Laura's pieces to Adam's modernist aesthetic that made the difference. An unfamiliar sage-green carpet complemented the curtains patterned with grape vines and small golden flowers now hanging in the living room. Adam had steadfastly rejected both floor and window coverings when he and Liz lived together; apparently he had mellowed with age.

Liz had never been fond of Adam's furniture, but since she'd moved from Prince Edward Island with nothing but a suitcase and picked up the bare minimum of student furnishings at second-hand stores, it was a big improvement over what she brought to their relationship. When Adam eventually moved out he'd taken his favourite pieces with him: the Eames lounge chair and ottoman, the black leather sofa she'd hated for its reptilian texture but endured for its practicality, the Saarinen table and matching tulip chairs evoking a paradoxically old-fashioned view of the future, something from *The Jetsons* or *2001: A Space Odyssey* — the kind of chairs used by people in candy-coloured jumpsuits living in a city of skyscrapers and monorails in a world without hunger or disease or corpses abandoned in parks.

Liz suddenly realized that she was sitting in one of those chairs with a steaming cup of tea in front of her. A pot of honey, a pretty ceramic jug of milk, and a plate of biscotti had also appeared.

"Thanks," she said.

"I thought you looked cold," said Laura. "Hunched over like that."

"I just came back from walking the dog and I guess I got chilled. It's starting to feel like winter."

"I love your Jasper. We always had dogs when I was growing up in São Paulo, but now I am away from home too much to take care of a pet."

"You could always have fish," Liz said.

Laura laughed. "Fish are not very cuddly."

"You'd be surprised. My friend Ronnie has a pond full of carp in her backyard and they swim right over to her to have their bellies tickled."

"It would be so interesting to have a relationship with a fish. Something so alien, and yet not. We have a lot in common with animals, no?"

"Well, maybe because you are a dancer you're more aware of the similarities than most people are. Because your art is non-verbal, I mean," said Liz. She liked this girl a lot more than she thought she would.

"Perhaps, yes. I think that you are correct. And also, living in another language makes it a big relief not to use words."

"But your English is great."

"Thank you. But still, too much of the time I am translating my thoughts from Portuguese, and it makes me tired. Sometimes I feel like my head is going to go boom."

"I don't want to make your head go boom, I just wanted to see Adam," Liz said, standing up to go. "Tell him to call me, okay? And thanks for the tea."

"Is there any way I can help?" asked Laura. "Is it about the kids?"

"Yes, it is. Well, about Samantha."

"That she is becoming very thin?"

"I didn't think dancers believed it was possible for anyone to be too thin," said Liz, sitting down again abruptly. Nice, smart, and observant! Clearly there was more to Adam's dancer than her stunning legs, which she'd managed to fold under her gracefully despite the awkward shape of the tulip chair.

"That was Balanchine's fault. He liked a certain type of

body — short torso, long limbs, very narrow — because it suited his choreography, which was all about extension, you know? Women were supposed to be like birds, or maybe angels." Her arms swept up, one in front and one behind her, to illustrate her point. "But now, things are changing. Myself, I would not enjoy dancing if I could never be strong onstage."

"I see," Liz said. And she did. She'd never thought about it before, but this must be the reason she'd always preferred modern dance to ballet. It seemed more human somehow; more grounded; more about emotions she could connect with and shapes her own muscles could relate to.

"But Samantha is not a ballerina, she is an athlete. And she will no longer be able to compete if she starves herself," Laura said.

"I've told her that but she won't listen to me. So I'm taking her to the doctor tomorrow."

"It must be the boyfriend."

"That's what Josh and I both think. And that's what I wanted Adam to talk to her about."

"At that age girls are very insecure, no? When my first boyfriend kept making comments about pretty blond actresses in American movies, I dyed my hair."

"And what happened?"

"I looked like a hooker."

"I mean, what happened with him?" Liz said, laughing.

"He dumped me anyway. Because I was always dancing, so I was not able to go to parties or stay out late. He said that being with me was no fun."

"My first boyfriend loved me just the way I was," said Liz

thoughtfully, "but who I was then is very different from who I am now. Very different from the person I *wanted* to be."

"So you felt that you must leave him so that you could change?" Laura asked.

"Yes, exactly. But to leave him I had to leave home as well. Everything there conspired to hold me back."

"Sometimes you cannot see yourself until you are in a new place. Like moving a painting or a piece of furniture."

"Speaking of which, I like what you've done with the flat. It was kind of bare before."

"Thank you, Liz. I wonder why Adam likes such cold things. He is a very warm person."

"It's part of being an art teacher, I think. Having good taste. He always insisted that his stuff wasn't cold, just 'uncluttered.'"

"But no colours anywhere? You can have colours without clutter," protested Laura.

"I'm with you. Anyhow, thanks for talking. I still don't know what to do about Sammy, but at least I know I'm not imagining things."

Liz got up to leave for a second time. Laura put a tentative arm out to stop her.

"Sometimes a girl will feel more comfortable talking to someone who is not her mother ..." she started to say, then hesitated.

"Are you offering to talk to her, Laura?"

"I'm sorry, it is none of my business," she said. Liz was amazed to see that she was blushing.

"No, no, don't apologize. It's very generous of you. In fact, I think it might be a good idea."

"Really?"

"Really. Why don't you talk it over with Adam and see what he thinks?"

"Thank you for trusting me. I know it must be hard for you, having me living upstairs like this. You are a good person."

"You too, Laura," Liz said, giving her a hug. "Which is a relief, given that you are part of my children's lives now."

"We are being very mature, no?" Laura said, hugging her back.

"Well, somebody has to be."

LIZ TRIED TO BE equally mature when she took Sammy to the doctor's office. Instead of fussing at her daughter on the way there, she asked questions about school activities and even encouraged disparagement of the new vice-principal, hated by all the students for his killjoy officiousness. She sat in the waiting room, pretending to read an article about Hepatitis C, and let her daughter be examined without maternal interference. When Samantha came out, trumpeting, "The doctor says I'm fine, just like I told you," Liz didn't argue but simply asked to have a word with the physician herself. He confirmed that Sammy had lost quite a bit of weight — eleven pounds as it turned out — since her last checkup. Nonetheless, her BMI was still in the normal range, if low, which was not unusual for a high school athlete. He conceded that if it got much lower, if Sammy continued to drop weight at the same rate, there might be cause to worry. But not yet.

The doctor's main concern was that Sammy get enough vitamin D and iron, so he did a blood test and suggested she start taking a multivitamin in the meantime. Liz wasn't satisfied with this result, but she recognized that she had done all she could for now. They stopped off at the pharmacy on the way home and tried to simulate an ordinary mother-daughter outing by trying on garish colours of eye shadow, spraying each other with perfume, flipping through trashy magazines, and buying completely unnecessary products such as a shower pouf in the shape of a bright red ladybug, a bottle of sky-blue nail polish, and some Spiderman Band-Aids for Josh. It was the most fun they'd had together in a long time.

MEANWHILE, JOSH HAD DECIDED to help his sister in his own way. This consisted mainly of exploiting Facebook. Because of all the sports he played and his various musical adventures, Josh had a wide network of friends and acquaintances and he was determined to use every connection he had to get the goods on his sister's boyfriend. He eventually found someone from his soccer team who knew Derek from middle school, where the boy had developed quite a reputation. The soccer player knew another guy who had gone to Derek's first high school with him, and also remembered the name of his second high school, way out in the west end, where Josh himself knew several students who had more recent information about him.

He'd compiled all this data with an exactitude his school assignments lacked. He presented his findings to his mother Sunday evening, when Sammy was out at a movie with Derek. Liz was in the kitchen making a salad and shouting out the answers to *Jeopardy!* Liz put down the carrot scraper, turned off the television, and peered at the blurry pages Josh waved in front of her. She had no idea where her reading glasses were.

"What is all this, Josh?"

"The dirt on Derek."

"Where did you get it?"

"You know how you're always warning us about compromising our privacy by using social media? Well, there's an upside to living your life in public. It makes it very easy to find out stuff about other people — including Derek Webster."

"What kind of stuff?" Liz's heart sank. As much as she mistrusted him, she had never suspected her daughter's boyfriend of anything truly reprehensible.

"Where would you like me to start? Despite having his face plastered all over fashion spreads for The Bay, he's never been a model citizen, our Derek. When he was in middle school he got busted for shoplifting CDs from a music store. Then at his first high school he moved to a higher level of crime — if you catch my drift — by selling drugs to another student."

Liz sat down heavily in a chair. She felt like she was going to faint. "This is much worse than I imagined."

"To be fair, it was only pot, Mum, and in pretty insignificant quantities. He wasn't a big-time dealer or anything. According to him, he wasn't selling drugs, just sharing them with friends. Still, after he got busted he was suspended for a week and then he transferred to another school."

"Is that it?" she asked hopefully.

"Not quite. At his second high school he got into a fight with another guy. He claimed the kid said Derek's mother dressed like a slut when she was wearing her waitress uniform. So he clocked him. Because of that school's zero tolerance policy, he landed with us. The school board doesn't expel problem kids anymore. It just moves them around."

"I'm sure Sammy has no idea about any of this or she never would have gone out with Derek in the first place." She took a deep breath. "Joshie, do you think she's in danger?"

"I doubt it. Derek's been walking the straight and narrow since he came to our school. He's constantly working out and never even touches junk food, much less drugs. Still, I think Sammy should know the truth about the guy she's dating, don't you?"

"Of course. But she's going to be so angry you spied on her boyfriend."

"I know, Mum. Which is why I was hoping you'd talk to her for me." Josh sat down beside Liz, crossed his arms on the table, and dropped his head onto them with a groan. Jasper, concerned, heaved himself up to stand by Josh's side.

"Jasper, what a good doggy you are. You talk to Sammy, okay?" Liz tried to sound jovial but the humour was forced, and Jasper recognized it. He gave a half-hearted wag of the tail, his eyes on Josh the whole time. Liz scratched the dog under his chin, and sighed.

"We'll figure something out. But I don't want to alienate Sammy. I feel like she's already slipping away from us. One of the universal rules of parenting is 'never criticize your daughter's boyfriend.'"

"Do you think I made a mistake digging this stuff up?"

"No. Not at all. I'm really grateful to you, sweetheart. And your sister will be too, one day. Just maybe not in my lifetime."

THOUGH SHE HAD LOST her own appetite for the salad she had just finished assembling, Liz watched her gangly son dump a can of tuna on his portion, empty half a box of croutons on top, slather the whole thing with about an inch of Caesar dressing, and wolf it down in five minutes.

"Gotta go, Mum. Sean and I are building a scale model of a theatre for architecture class. It's way cool. You should see it." Having unburdened himself of the bad news about Derek, he easily recovered his habitual cheerfulness. Apparently, he still believed his mother could fix everything. If only she believed it herself.

"I'd love to see your project, Josh. Maybe you guys could work on it over here next time?"

"We can't move the model. It's too fragile. And anyhow, Sean has more space than we do, so his folks don't mind if we spread everything out and just leave it until we're finished."

"Do they have a big house?" She felt a pang, as she always did whenever she wondered if her children were embarrassed to be living above a store.

"No, it's pretty small, but his older sister is away at university, so we're using her bedroom as our workshop."

"Ah." Another pang. One more year and then both her kids might be away at university themselves. Would life be harder or easier when she no longer had any idea what they were up to?

LIZ CONTINUED TO SIT at the table, Josh's dossier on the petty crimes of Derek Webster in front of her, icy fingers clamped on her heart. How could she tell her sweet trusting daughter that the boy she idolized, her first real love, was not who he pretended to be? "The first cut is the deepest," went the old saying, and Liz knew how true that was from her own experience. It had taken her more than a year to break up with Paul Donnelly back on the island; a year during which their parents were happily compiling the guest list for a big church wedding; a year during which she went to bed each night afraid to voice her doubts to the boy who had loved her faithfully since grade ten, the only boy who had ever loved her and whom everyone — including Liz's own mother — considered too good to be true. Nice-looking, polite, all set to be an optician like his father.

The way her mother idolized Paul had irritated Liz, but it was the pleasure Paul took in playing bridge with his parents every weekend that filled her heart with dread; that and his practice of counting steps out loud during slow dances. And the little flourish with which he placed his napkin on his lap before eating, and how he dabbed his mouth with it after almost every bite. And the way he said "anywho" instead of "anyhow" and his habit of introducing her as "my intended." And at least a dozen other idiosyncrasies that would have gone unremarked — or at least uncriticized — by anyone in love, which she clearly wasn't. She'd tolerated much worse behaviour from Adam when his time came.

Despite her conviction that she was saving herself from a life of stultifying dullness, breaking up with Paul was the hardest thing she had ever done. She practically fled the island in disgrace. But Sammy's relationship with Derek was relatively new, there really was no comparison, and the way her daughter was behaving these days suggested that things between them weren't going all that well. So maybe, deep down, Sammy would be glad of an excuse to break things off. She'd be angry, but she'd also be relieved.

Liz picked up the phone and then put it down again. Adam was home; she'd heard his footsteps going up the stairs. She knew she should talk to him right away but hesitated, knowing how enraged he would become. Heavy parental interference would only drive Sammy away, of that she was sure; just as sure as she was that Adam would never be able to control himself when it came to somebody taking advantage of his daughter. But she didn't have the strength to deal with this on her own. She was too upset to be rational.

Luckily, Laura had offered to help. Beautiful young Laura, cool hip Laura; Laura who was definitely not one of Sammy's parents. All Liz had to do was to wait until morning and then, once Adam had gone off to work, she and Laura could figure out a plan of action. It shouldn't be too hard to hide her concerns in the meantime. All she had to do was take refuge in the bathtub when Sammy returned, then take Jasper for a walk, and finally go to bed early, feigning a headache. It was unlikely Sammy would suspect that anything was wrong, given how rarely she talked to her mother these days.

Liz started running the bath, hoping it would calm her down as well as keep her from confronting her daughter. Maybe she'd pour in one of the aromatherapy oils her daughter had given her for her birthday, back in the summer, back when Sammy was still talking to her. Liz hadn't sampled them. She wondered why she always saved nice things for a rainy day.

As soon as she opened the box a wave of scent hit her. Five little bottles with pretty labels and a booklet on how to use them. She flipped through it quickly, reading about the properties of each bottle and then opening each stopper in turn to take a sniff. Neither vanilla nor peppermint appealed to her in the least. Why would anyone want to smell like a bakery? And citrus was too lively for the way she was feeling right now; it was clearly a wake-up-energized-in-the-morning kind of aroma. Rose was too romantic, too wide-eyed and young. Not disillusioned enough, somehow. But lavender felt just right: delicate, old-fashioned, kind of sad and quaint. Bruised, like she was. Besides, the label said it was meant to relieve stress. So she poured an extravagant amount into the bubbling water, threw her dirty clothes in the laundry hamper, and enjoyed the unexpected pleasure of walking down the hall naked in her own house.

Hearing a key in the lock, she scurried back hastily to the bathroom.

"I'm home," Sammy yelled.

"I'm taking a bath, sweetheart," Liz shouted back. "How was the movie?"

"It was okay. The acting sucked, but the special effects were phenomenal."

"Do you need supper? There's a salad in the fridge, and some good whole grain bread and cheese."

"No thanks, we had lots of popcorn. I'm stuffed."

"Really?" She couldn't help herself, even with the bathroom door between them.

"God, Mum, give it a rest," Sammy snapped.

"Okay. See you later."

There was no reply. A few minutes later, she heard the sound of the teakettle whistling followed shortly by the sound of Sammy marching down the hall to her room. She slammed the door more loudly than necessary. Liz lay back in the steaming tub and shut her eyes. "Do your work, lavender," she prayed. "I'm counting on you."

10

MONDAY MORNING, AFTER GEORGIA arrived at the bookstore, Liz went upstairs to talk to Laura. Laura was less upset than she was about the information Josh had unearthed, which was to be expected. What surprised Liz, however, was how compassionate the other woman was about the boy's situation.

"Don't you feel sorry for Derek?" Laura said. "He is trying so hard to change himself. Like going out with Sammy — a good girl and a serious student. Not the kind of person a drug dealer would be attracted to. Perhaps he did not tell your daughter about his past because he thought she would not like him anymore if she knew what he had done."

"But that's even worse. How dare someone with his record try to make my daughter feel inadequate?"

"Why do you say that?"

"He's always boasting about his accomplishments and post-ing videos of himself on YouTube."

"He is probably just as insecure as Sammy is."

"Sammy never used to be insecure," Liz protested. "She's always been the most confident, opinionated, bossy little person I know."

"But has she ever had a boyfriend before?"

"I don't think so. Frankly, it's hard to tell, the way they all hang out in a mob these days."

Laura laughed. She was wearing a heathery green sweater that matched her eyes and emphasized the startling contrast between them and her glossy black hair. And silver bangles. And matching earrings. And makeup.

Liz suddenly realized that Laura had dressed up for their meeting. She had to admit that in honour of this historic occasion she too had paid more attention to her appearance than usual, although nothing short of plastic surgery could make her look as good as Laura. But at least her shirt was clean, as were her nails. And her own hair, while not as lustrous as Laura's, was still beautiful and thick and naturally blond. She shook her head unconsciously and felt the soft weight of it settle around her shoulders.

"You would be aware if she had fallen in love before, Liz. Besides, you know how self-conscious teenage girls are, especially about their bodies. It is not the boy's fault that Sammy wants to please him. That time I told you about, when I dyed my hair blond, my boyfriend said he liked it much better when it was dark and couldn't understand why I would change it."

"Maybe you're right. But it's hard for me to be objective when it comes to my daughter. I can't help wanting to swat the little weasel."

"Derek may be a little weasel, but you are a fierce mother bear." Laura laughed again.

"Okay, fine, I admit it. But she's my baby and I don't want her to get hurt." That laugh was starting to irritate her. Laura didn't seem to be taking the situation seriously enough.

"No one gets through life without being hurt," Laura continued, as though thinking aloud. "It is natural to want to protect your daughter, but Samantha is almost a woman and soon she'll leave home. Then what will you do?"

"I don't know, but right now, while she's still under my roof, I have to do what I can. It's my job, Laura. You'll understand one day when you have kids."

"I have had one child already, Liz. And no matter how hard I tried, I was not able to protect her."

"I'm so sorry; I had no idea ..." Liz was mortified.

"How could you know? Unless Adam told you."

"No, he hasn't told me much about you. I know that you're a dancer, and that you come from Brazil, and that you two are travelling through Southeast Asia together. That's about it." Liz paused, feeling like she was about to jump off a cliff. "What happened to your daughter, Laura?"

"Leukemia. She died when she was four, before we could get a bone marrow transplant. Children usually have a good survival rate for leukemia, but Allegra was not one of the lucky ones."

"Oh my God, when did this happen?"

"Four years ago. My husband Ricardo and I split up not long after that. We could not forgive each other for her death. I blamed him for not looking after her properly; he blamed me for not giving up my career to stay home with Allegra. There was so much anger. It was easier for us to be angry with each other than to accept what had happened."

She paused and brushed her hand across her eyes. "A year later I came to Toronto to visit a cousin. She convinced me to move here. Toronto seemed like a good place to start over. There was nothing for me back home but guilt."

"It wasn't your fault she got sick, Laura."

"But if I'd been home more maybe I would have noticed that something was wrong with my baby. I would have had more time with her. We had so little time."

Both women were silent. Liz made some rapid calculations: Laura had given birth eight years ago; she had been married; she'd had a whole complicated grown-up life already. It didn't seem possible — she looked so young.

"How old are you, Laura? I thought you were just in your twenties."

"I turned thirty-three in September. How old are you?"

"Forty-four. But despite my extra years, I haven't had to suffer what you have. I can't even imagine it. I am so, so sorry."

Liz reached out and grasped Laura's hand, which was warmly given. What she was facing with Samantha was *nothing*, nothing at all, just part of the ordinary business of growing up. Sammy was safe, she would get through this; they all would.

LAURA AGREED TALK TO Sammy. Liz went downstairs to work in the bookstore but found herself unable to think about anything except Laura's daughter, Allegra. Cancer was supposed to kill people like Liz's father, middle-aged men who were heavy smokers, people with a big whack of living already behind them, not four-year-old girls. Certainly at four Sammy had seemed indestructible, throwing her compact little body into every possible activity with an astonishing lack of fear. At four, Sammy didn't worry about dying; she worried about the homeless people on the street and wanted to bring them blankets and hot chocolate. At four, Sammy planned to be a scientist, a ballerina, and a cupcake baker — to save the world, entertain it, and feed it, all at the same time. At four, Sammy had promised to live with her mother forever and ever. How would Liz have survived if she had lost her?

You could love your child devotedly, inoculate her against every disease known to man, breastfeed her, make her homemade baby food, never let her outside without sunscreen and a hat, and she could *still* get cancer. Liz knew these things in the abstract; she wasn't stupid. But facing the reality, as Laura had, was inconceivable to her.

"There really is no safe place, Jasper," Liz said. "Being alive is a very dangerous business."

The dog looked up at her, wagged his tail, and then stretched out on his back for a belly rub. Liz leaned over and obligingly raked her fingers through his thick pelt wishing — not for the first time — that her life were as simple as his, her needs as primal, her spirit as light. Finding James Scott's body in Wychwood Park had shaken her trust in the world. The subsequent vandalism of the bookstore had increased her sense of being under threat; learning about Derek's misadventures was leading her to outright panic. She hadn't realized that her response might be extreme until Laura reminded her that plenty of kids get into trouble with the law and still turn out fine.

Liz knew that was true. In fact, the biggest troublemaker in her own school back on the island, a boy everyone predicted was headed for prison, was now a high school principal, and the disgraced girl who had a baby in grade eleven had gone on to law school and become a passionate and articulate advocate for women's rights. So shouldn't she give Derek another chance? Shouldn't she trust Sammy to choose someone who would be good to her? Had she herself been so successful in love that she could judge what was best for other people?

Her brooding was interrupted by six talkative browsers, only one of whom actually bought a book; the postman; the UPS guy with a special order for a customer who collected all kinds of odd things and had amassed an eclectic library of resource material, the current example being an auction guide to daguerreotypes; and finally by Max. He arrived, gentleman that he was, with a couple of flaky *pains au chocolat* in a paper bag.

"How did you know I was in desperate need of something sweet?" Liz asked.

"It's a pretty safe bet with you, my dear. Is this a convenient time to take a break?"

"Sure. I'm getting nothing done anyway."

"What's the matter? Are you still worried about your daughter?"

"More than ever. So much has happened in the past couple

of days, Max. Do you want tea while we eat these and talk? Or would you prefer coffee?"

"Coffee for me, thanks. It goes better with chocolate."

"Everything goes better with chocolate, Max. It's like O negative is the universal donor."

They walked into the little kitchenette at the back of the store and Liz brought Max up-to-date. In a mad rush, full of digressions and self-recriminations, she told him what Josh had found out about Derek and how she had reacted, and then how Laura had reacted and what she had learned about Laura, and how ashamed she now was of herself. Recognizing the panic in her voice, Max turned the conversation to Internet research — a topic that he knew was unfailingly interesting to her and therefore a surefire diversion.

"I must say, I'm very impressed with your son's detective skills. Do you think that we should try to find James Scott on this Facebook thing?"

"No. According to everyone who knew him he never revealed anything private, which is basically all that people do on Facebook. To be honest, it worries me how much strangers can find out about my kids that way. They keep insisting that their security settings are impregnable, but I don't trust the Internet."

"Well, they're a different generation with different notions of privacy. I would imagine that even James Scott was too old for that."

"Probably. But I'm running out of ideas about what else to do. We can't post a random message asking 'Anybody who knows anything about the late James Scott, please contact this number,' can we?"

"I'm sure the police have already done something like that and they have much better resources than we do."

"Max," Liz said slowly, "you just gave me an idea. What if we aren't the only people who were looking for information about James Scott?"

"What do you mean?"

"Well, what if somebody else was looking for him and finally found him. Somebody he was hiding from? Somebody who hated him enough to kill him? I only searched 'James Scott'; I didn't search 'Looking for James Scott.' Let's give it a whirl."

Max swallowed a last mouthful of coffee, rinsed his mug in the sink, and went out to Liz's desk where she was already scrolling down through computer entries at a speed that impressed him.

"Bingo." Her distress had been replaced by the thrill of the hunt, and there was a fanatic gleam in her eye. "Last July there was a missing-persons inquiry on the Sault Ste. Marie Craigslist that says: 'Looking for Andrew James Scott, born 1977, foster son of the McKay family in Ste. Anne in 1989. Urgent that I find him!' It's signed 'Brian McKay.'"

"Not son, but *foster* son. Perhaps Mr. Scott has so little online history because he lacked conventional family ties."

"You could be right."

"But what is Craig's list? I've never heard of it."

"Craigslist is a free online bulletin board where people can post events and list items to buy and sell. I've used the Toronto one to find second-hand furniture. After Adam took back his kitchen table and chairs I bought my new ones that way. You've seen them — they're really nice, good quality oak. Each Craigslist is pretty much a local thing, so this particular Ste. Anne must be somewhere near Sault Ste. Marie."

She pulled an atlas from a shelf.

"I was right. It's in the same neighbourhood as Espanola, Manitoulin, Kagawong, Blind River, Killarney, and Thessalon. It's a regular United Nations up there."

"I wonder why someone named an Ontario town Thessalon? Maybe because it is in the north, like Thessalonika is in Greece."

"Maybe," said Liz, still studying the map.

"Thessalonika was named after the sister of Alexander the Great, you know," Max continued.

"How would I know something like that? Oh, you're really going to love this, Max. There's a Thessalon First Nation. What could be more Canadian than a First Nations community named after a city in Greece named after Alexander the Great's sister?"

"They're not the first Indians to be associated with Alexander. His empire once stretched as far as the Punjab."

"And I thought I already knew all the trivia I would ever need in this lifetime! But while we're on the topic of names, do you really think this can be the right Mr. Scott? His first name is Andrew."

"Why not? Many people change their names unofficially. My own wife did. The name on her birth certificate was Tatiana but she always went by Tanya, even on her driver's licence."

"Actually, now that I think about it, my friend Melanie's first name was really Agnes but she hated it, so as soon as she left home she went by her second name instead. Scott could have done exactly the same thing, Max, just dropped the Andrew and called himself James."

"I wonder how we can find out."

"Well, one thing is for sure. I can't write to this Brian McKay and say: 'Hello there, person I don't know. The party you are looking for, if he ditched his first name, might be a dead guy I accidentally stumbled upon in Toronto in October.'"

"That would be awkward, I admit. But what else can we do?"

"I guess I could try to dig up more information, this time looking up both Andrew James Scott and Brian McKay."

"How about if you keep on researching Mr. Scott, since you've spent so much time with him already, and I'll pursue Mr. McKay," Max suggested. "We can compare notes tomorrow or the next day."

"Okay. Laura and I still have to confront Sammy tonight about the unsavoury stuff Josh dug up on her beloved Derek. You have no idea how much I'm dreading it."

"*Bon courage*," said Max. "It will be difficult. But make it clear to your daughter how much you love her and I'm sure everything will turn out fine."

BUT EVERYTHING DID NOT turn out fine. It was only Laura's watchful presence that kept Sammy from having a complete meltdown — something she'd been expert at since the age of one, when she'd occasionally held her breath so long she started to turn blue. Even with Laura there, she and Liz were practically screaming in each other's faces from the start.

"Why do you always treat me like I'm an idiot?"

"Nobody is treating you like an idiot, Samantha. That's why we're trying to have an adult conversation with you," said Laura.

"Oh yeah? How many adults have people gang up on them to diss their boyfriends?"

"Adults whose friends worry about them," Liz said.

"This is all Josh's fault. I can't believe he would do something like this. I'm never speaking to him again, I swear."

"But Sammy, he was only trying to protect you. He thought you would want to know the truth about Derek."

"I already *knew* all this stuff, Mum, I just didn't tell you because I knew you would automatically condemn him without hearing the whole story."

"What whole story?"

"It's no big deal. Derek got into a little trouble when his parents split up. Lots of kids do! You complained when I failed one stupid math exam after Daddy moved out but you had no idea what else was going on."

"What do you mean?" Liz felt her pulse accelerate. What had she missed?

"I did some shoplifting back then. Mostly lip gloss and chocolate bars from the drugstore. Crap like that."

Liz gasped, but Sammy continued, undeterred. In fact, she seemed to be enjoying the effect this revelation was having on her mother.

"The most valuable thing I stole was a pair of silver earrings. Those dangly ones you like, with the garnets in them. I said they were a present from Daddy. You were so mad at him that ended the conversation."

"Oh, Sammy. Why would you do something like that?"

"I was angry. I felt deprived. Whatever."

"What do you mean, 'whatever'? You know how much I hate that expression." Liz knew she was grasping at straws to regain her authority but she couldn't help herself.

"Didn't you take Psych 100 in university? Just be glad I wasn't cutting myself like some of my friends."

"Some of your friends *cut* themselves?" Liz was stunned. She felt she had just tipped over into an alternative universe. Her daughter's friends seemed so well-adjusted; they worked hard at school and were busy with extracurricular activities so they could get into good universities. How was it possible that behind that facade of wholesomeness there was so much pain?

"You only see what you want to see, Mum. That's why you love saying you live in Hillcrest Village instead of at Christie and St. Clair. So you can pretend this is Ye Olde England, all quaint and cozy."

"What about the drugs, Sammy? Derek sold drugs," Liz insisted, trying to hold on to her righteous anger in the face of increasing guilt and confusion.

"He did not! He was trying to get into a band and the drummer asked him to score some weed as a sort of initiation test, to see how cool he was. He brought the dope to school like a complete idiot and got busted."

"Are you sure that's what really happened?" She tried to keep her voice neutral, but Samantha remained furious anyway.

"Yes, I'm sure. And why are you being so self-righteous all of a sudden? You're always pretending to be hip and non-judgmental. But it's really just an act, isn't it?"

"It's only that I'm worried about you. You're still my little girl, Sammy."

"Number one: I'm not little anymore. And number two: Derek's my boyfriend. So you'd better get used to it," she shouted over her shoulder as she slammed the door.

Liz sank onto the sofa with her head in her hands. Laura sat down beside her; as usual, she was laughing. Jasper looked back and forth from one woman to the other, confused as to which emotion was dominant. He whimpered in distress until Liz put out one hand to pat him and whispered, "Shhh."

"Don't worry, Liz," Laura said. "When she walks off her anger, she will be ready to talk to you."

"I wish I believed you."

"Didn't you ever fight with your mother?"

"No. In my family, we didn't fight. We just sulked in our rooms until it was time for a meal. Then we sat in silence, listening to each other chew. At least, that was how it was until I broke up with the man my mother wanted me to marry. A few harsh words were exchanged then, I have to admit."

"But you made up."

"Eventually. But I was already living away from home by then. Also, I was a different type of person than my daughter is. I was much less dramatic, for one thing."

"But that is exactly why Sammy will come around. Her emotions are right on the surface. She cannot hold anything inside for long. You will see."

"I hope you're right, Laura," Liz sighed. "Meanwhile, I'm curious. What are you going to say to Adam about all this?"

"Nothing. We have no reason to tell Adam that Derek got

into a little trouble in his previous high school."

"Thank you," said Liz. "That's definitely the best approach to take."

Liz showed Laura to the door, relieved not to have to discuss Derek's juvenile record with Adam. She was sure Sammy didn't need another person criticizing her love life — especially her doting father, who would probably want to shoot Derek on sight.

HE DISCOVERED he was a natural salesman. This didn't surprise him; he sort of expected that he would be. Except for his own father, who left when he was a baby, and his mother's boyfriend, who enjoyed burning him with cigarettes, and Brian, who he tried very hard not to think about, all his life folks had tended to like him and to trust him on sight. He'd noticed this during his days in juvenile detention and then in construction: a surprising number of people wanted to be his friend. He hoped that meant there was still some goodness left in him.

He was pretty sure he wasn't born bad. His mother said that he had been an angel-baby: chubby, blond, and sweet-natured, a child who made everyone smile. He didn't think he was bad when she still had a job and he went to daycare during the week and on weekends they went to the park and were happy. Maybe he caught being bad from her drinking the way second-hand smoke gave people cancer, or maybe it was beaten into him by her boyfriend, who hated him from day one. Anyway, as long as he kept the badness hidden deep inside him where no one else could see it, he would be fine. Nice suits, nice car, and nice manners: most people trusted appearances.

He did look good. The ladies loved him and, although he never let anyone get too close emotionally, he loved sex. It was fun, and it allowed him some human warmth without endangering his precarious sense of identity. Oddly enough, this reluctance to let people get too close just made the ladies want him more. It was a "win-win situation," as his boss at the real estate agency said about their practice of underpricing houses to ensure that they would be subject to bidding wars. Because he never tried too hard, women didn't feel threatened by him. And because he always held something back, they were willing to give him more than he asked for.

There was one girl he genuinely liked: Natalie, a secretary at the family law partnership on the same floor as his real estate agency. She came from a small town he'd never heard of somewhere in New Brunswick and was completely bilingual. This impressed him, although working in Toronto he'd met plenty of women more successful and ambitious than her. So that wasn't it. Nor was she the prettiest or even the most glamorous girl around. But whenever he talked to her he felt like she was totally there, in the moment, not thinking of anything else, just steadily taking him in with her candid brown eyes. They often chatted in the hall and on the elevator and had gone out for coffee a couple of times after work, and he could tell she liked him too.

Maybe she was someone he could get close to? He was almost thirty and he was tired of hiding. He wanted to be with a woman who would accept him for who he was. But how could he ever tell the truth about himself to someone like her? Someone who spoke about her own family with such tenderness and still wrote letters to her grandmother and knit hats and booties for the baby niece whose photograph she showed him with unaffected delight?

Someone good.

Because Natalie had such a kind heart, she might be able to forgive him. But that wasn't what he wanted from her. He didn't want to be pitied or forgiven; he didn't want to be seen as damaged goods. He was afraid that if he told her who he really was her eyes would well up as they did when she talked about some of the sad cases she heard about at work. And he'd already been a sad case for too much of his life.

11

Liz had a pounding headache. No. The headache had Liz. She was held captive while it snarled at her that she was stupid and naïve and had no idea what was really going on around her. She might be able to read a book a day but she was illiterate when it came to people. "You only see what you want to see, Mum," Sammy had said. Was this why Liz was a failure as a wife and a mother? Would her children grow up to have contempt for her? Who was she kidding; they already had contempt for her.

All she had wanted was a life in which Sunday's roast was not recycled as Monday's shepherd's pie; a life that didn't smell like floor wax; a life in which her shoes did not have to match her purse. She hadn't asked for fame or fortune or exotic vacations, just some decent conversation and the possibility that her children could grow up to be citizens of a larger world. But she was a hypocrite, because that larger world scared her to death. In that world perfectly nice men were murdered and disposed of casually in public parks. In that world, vandals smashed shop windows just for fun. In that world, her lovely daughter became anorexic and her daughter's boyfriend dealt drugs to be accepted in high school. In that larger world, children cut themselves with razor blades to express their rage and grief.

Liz gulped a fistful of ibuprofen and lay down on the sofa, praying for sleep. But sleep did not come. Wave after wave of shame washed over her. She felt guilty for all the times she'd made fun of her neurotic mother; guilty for all the times she'd congratulated herself on how oblivious her children were to junk food and junk culture; guilty for boasting about the civilized relationship she and Adam had maintained after their divorce. She'd been so busy patting herself on the back for escaping her small-town roots she'd failed to notice that this carefully constructed existence was just a stage set, like her quaint little bookstore. She wasn't a Bohemian, for God's sake; she was a librarian. She was as addicted to order as her poor mother, and just as afraid of spontaneity and risk.

The ringing of the phone cut through her head like a chainsaw. She wished she could just let it go to voicemail, but Josh wasn't home yet so she had to answer it. She might be a lousy mother, but she was a mother nonetheless.

"Liz, I know we said we'd wait until tomorrow, but do you have a minute to talk now?" It was Max, sounding excited.

"Why not? Pretty soon you'll be the only person talking to me."

"I'm being inconsiderate to call you at a time like this."

"It's okay, Max. I need something to take my mind off this business with Samantha. What's up?"

"I couldn't find anything about the McKay family online, so I went to the reference library. I thought they might be able to help me access some newspapers from northern Ontario, but there was nothing in their archives or even on the *Canadian Newsstand* database. So the librarian suggested that I search the *Toronto Star* database instead. She reasoned that if anything really important had happened involving the McKay family, it might make the papers in the big city too."

"And?"

"And up popped an obituary for Adèle McKay, born Adèle Marie Montclair in Toronto in 1939, who died tragically in a house fire in Ste. Anne in 1989. It says that she was survived by husband Charles and son Brian, but there's no mention of a foster child named Andrew James Scott."

"Maybe they just left him out," Liz replied wearily. She loved Max, but his enthusiasm was exhausting. He might not have anything else important going on in his life right now, but she did. How could she tell him so without being unforgivably rude?

"That isn't exactly what happened."

"What do you mean?"

"The obituary also included the date of Adèle McKay's funeral and the name of a funeral home. I called the funeral home."

"Max!"

"I'm an old man, Liz. I don't have time to waste and I don't care what people think of me anymore."

"But what did you say to the people at the funeral home?" Despite herself, she was becoming interested.

"I claimed to be investigating some outstanding details pertaining to the death of Adèle McKay of Ste. Anne back in 1989. Believe it or not, the same family still runs the place, so the father got on the line. He's retired, but he still likes to come in to work. Luckily for us he enjoys talking, so I found out everything I needed to know."

"Maxime Bertrand, I have a terrible migraine and you are making it worse. What did you learn?"

"That a foster child named Andrew James Scott confessed to the arson that burned down the McKay's house and killed Brian McKay's mother."

She gasped at the image that flared up in front of her: a tidy white clapboard house on fire, orange flames leaping into the sky. A little boy standing motionless in front of it with a box of matches in his hand. She could see the matches clearly: *Redbird Strike Anywhere* matches, the same kind her father used to light his cigarettes. The acrid smell of smoke filled her nostrils and screams of terror filled her ears.

Max's voice dispelled this vision. She shuddered, and returned to reality.

"Liz, I don't think it can be a coincidence that this fellow happened to be looking for someone named Scott, whom he had good reason to hate, a couple of months before you found someone named Scott murdered in Toronto."

"No, you're right. We should take this information to the detective in charge of the case. I still have his card somewhere. But he is going to be really pissed off because he made me promise not to do any investigating on my own."

"Well, you didn't find this out, Liz. I did. And as I told you before, I'm not concerned about what other people think, so just blame everything on me."

"Whatever you want. I'm too tired to think anymore. It's been a very, very long day."

"As Homer reminds us, 'there is a time for many words, and there is also a time for sleep.' *Bonne nuit*, Liz."

"Sweet dreams, Max."

LAURA WAS WRONG. SAMMY did not walk off her anger. On the contrary, she came back just as furious as when she left; perhaps more so, having had additional time to brood upon her mother's injustice and her brother's perfidy. Claiming she would never ever forgive either of them, she stomped right upstairs to Adam's flat, sending an apologetic Laura down a few minutes later to retrieve her laptop, homework, and a few personal items, including her special squishy pillow. Both kids kept a stash of clothes and toiletries at their father's place because they did stay there from time to time, so Sammy could manage for quite a while, and she could always sneak downstairs for supplies when nobody else was around. Knowing this, Liz was despondent. How could she persuade her daughter to come home?

She supposed she could write her an apology, although maybe that was too old-fashioned. It would probably be better to make her a mixtape because Sammy loved music so much. There must be lots of songs she could use, like that old chestnut her dad used to sing when he tracked mud into the kitchen:

"Who's Sorry Now?" Or what about Elton John's "Sorry Seems to Be the Hardest Word," or the Paul McCartney one that goes "We're So Sorry, Uncle Albert," although that wasn't really appropriate, was it? She should probably Google song titles with "forgive me" in them. Or she could just ask Josh; he was an encyclopedia of pop music and would know what kinds of tunes Sammy would like. They could make the tape together as a family project, the way they used to work on scrapbooks and dioramas when the kids were in elementary school. How she longed for the innocence of those days! Alternatively, they could stand at Adam's door and serenade her with "Baby Come Back."

But even as she told Josh her plan and they had a good laugh about it, Liz knew deep down that nothing would work. Her daughter was no longer a toddler having a temper tantrum that would pass like a summer storm, leaving her cheeks streaked with tears but her face sunny and bright. She was a young woman with a legitimate grievance who couldn't be tickled out of her indignation or bribed with strawberry ice cream to forget what had happened.

"Don't worry, Mum," Josh consoled her. "She'll cool off eventually. First of all, your cooking is way better than Dad's, even if she doesn't eat much of it. Secondly, she's going to feel like an intruder there because of Laura. And thirdly, even if she's mad at both of us, she's going to miss Jasper too much to stay away for long."

"I hope you're right. But I handled this badly, Josh. I criticized her boyfriend, so of course she defended him. What else could she do?"

"Admit the guy is a loser?"

"What girl would ever admit that about a boy she was going out with? No, I should have invited Derek over for a meal and then asked probing questions about his past."

"That would have been worse."

"Well, all I know is that there must have been a better alternative than confronting her head-on the way I did."

"Maybe," Josh admitted. "I've never seen her this angry before. Even when I cut all the hair off her Barbie doll."

"I'm serious, Joshua. You can't make me feel better by compulsive joking."

"Sorry."

"And what's worse is that I feel like I let her down again. I can't believe I was so oblivious to how she was feeling when Daddy and I split up. Did you know she was shoplifting?"

"Everyone shoplifts at least once in their lifetime, Mum."

"Please don't tell me you've shoplifted too!"

"Okay. I won't."

JOSH WENT OFF TO practise with his band, leaving Liz to wonder what other secrets her lighthearted son had been hiding from her. She knew he smoked a little pot on the weekends; after all, he was the lead guitarist in a rock band and she wasn't stupid, she knew dope was a big part of the music scene just as it had been a big part of the art scene when she first started going out with Adam, before they'd moved on to vintage wine and stinky cheeses.

She was also aware that Josh had tried cigarettes when he

was fourteen but had given them up quickly because his soccer coach said anyone he caught smoking would be kicked off the team with no second chances. Thank you, Soccer Coach. As far as she could tell he wasn't a big drinker, didn't gamble, wasn't addicted to porn, and hadn't gotten anyone pregnant, but she was beginning to realize how little she actually knew about what her kids were doing when they weren't with her. Of course, they spent so much time on their laptops that even when they were home they weren't really with her. She often felt like saying, "Get off that damn computer this minute!" But how could she? It was a way of life for them the way reading under the covers at night had been for her. It served the same purpose: creating a space away from parents for forging one's own identity.

She was about to take Jasper for a long walk, figuring she might as well put all this maternal anxiety to good use, when Adam pounded on the door, distraught, demanding to know what the hell was going on. He'd just walked in on Laura consoling his weeping daughter and when he'd asked why Sammy was so upset, they'd told him to mind his own business.

"I see," said Liz, in a tired voice. Another party heard from.

"I may not be your husband anymore, Liz, but I will always be Sammy's father, and I have just as much right to be involved in her life as you do. You can't shut me out."

"Nobody is trying to shut you out, Adam."

"Then how come Laura knows more about what's going on than I do? And since when did the two of you become so chummy?"

"We're not exactly chummy, but I have to say I like her, Adam. She's a really substantial person."

"Why thank you, Ms. Ryerson. Don't sound so surprised."

"I didn't mean to imply that I was surprised."

"Well, it sounded like you expected anyone I went out with to be an airhead. Which is kind of bizarre, considering that I used to be married to you."

Now she had managed to hurt everybody's feelings today. Not that she cared if Adam was offended, but she couldn't take any more recriminations.

"Look, Adam, I'm sorry if I misspoke. It's been a really bad week."

"Just tell me what's going on, Liz. What is Sammy so upset about?"

Liz sighed. "Did you know that she has a new boyfriend named Derek?"

"Yes, she showed me a video of him playing guitar on You-Tube. Pretty talented, I thought. He's also some kind of an actor, right?"

"Apparently. Well, Sammy and I had a little … disagreement about her relationship with him, and she just needs some time away from me to cool off."

"Is she sleeping with him? I'll kill the bastard."

"No, nothing like that, it's just mother-daughter stuff. So I'd really appreciate it if you let Sammy stay with you and Laura for a few days until she calms down."

"All right, but you know Laura and I are going away as soon as I get my final grades in. I don't want Sammy living alone in my place once we're gone, so you two had better work things out before then."

"Adam, how can you complain that I shut you out of your

daughter's life and then be resentful when I ask you to let her stay with you?" Liz said. "Did it ever occur to you that maybe you're the one shutting her out?"

"Give me a break, Liz. Why do you think I stayed in this building instead of moving into a place with a nice view and parking, a place where my ex-wife wouldn't glare at me every time I brought a girlfriend over? I stayed here for the kids and you know it, so don't give me that bullshit."

Jasper had started to whine. He needed to go out — or at least get away from their argument.

She knew exactly how he felt.

"Oh, forget it, Adam. I shouldn't have said anything; there's just way too much stress in my life right now."

"You know, when I met you I thought you were such a gentle, reflective person; I thought life with you would be so civilized after the screaming melodrama I grew up with. But you've changed."

"Well, when I married you I thought you'd be faithful. So let's just move on with our lives as they are now, shall we? Come on, Jasper," she said, elbowing past the father of her children and down the stairs. "Time for a walk."

She heard Adam close the door to her flat and go back up to his own, but she didn't turn around. The last thing she needed was for him to see her crying.

12

IT WAS EASIER THAN anticipated to connect with Detective Sergeant Keith Wentworth. Liz and Max made a date with him for Wednesday afternoon, when Georgia could take over at the bookstore again. The weather was unseasonably mild; one of those November days when the leaves have already fallen but the ground is bare of snow and the grass still patchily green, so that it's hard to tell whether it's autumn or somehow, miraculously missing winter, spring. Unfortunately, the police station's thermostat had not registered the change in temperature and the radiators were going full blast. Wentworth's shirt sleeves were rolled up and tie loosened and his window was propped open on a stack of out-of-date telephone books. He looked hot, frazzled, and not in the least pleased to see them.

"Well?" he said, his face more severe and older-looking than Liz remembered. Of course, the last time she met him she had been a shocked and innocent witness and he had been very solicitous, whereas today he was clearly annoyed by her presence. He'd immediately seen through the subterfuge that her dear friend, the renowned Professor Maxime Bertrand, might have some useful information about the case, and reproached Liz for doing independent research in spite of his asking her not to.

"What kind of professor are you, sir?"

"I taught classical literature for forty years."

"Please don't be offended, but how does a knowledge of Latin and Greek poetry qualify you to help with a homicide investigation?" The hostility was out in the open.

"My specialty was Greek tragedy, and I can assure you that it's as full of blood and guts as the most graphic cop show on television today. But what brought me here is something much more up-to-date. The Internet. Did you know that the murder victim's first name was actually Andrew and not James?"

"Yes. We learned that immediately from his driver's licence, his health card, and his birth certificate."

"And did you know that he had been a foster child?"

"How did you find that out? Child and Family Service records are supposed to be confidential." In spite of himself, Detective Wentworth was clearly interested; he was leaning forward, holding a pen in his hand as if poised to take notes.

"A missing person's ad online," said Max, handing over the printout from Craigslist.

"I see." Wentworth scanned the page. "I can't believe we missed something as obvious as this."

"When Max showed it to me, I knew we had to come to you right away, Detective Wentworth," Liz burst in, unable to hold back her excitement.

"Cicero said that the first duty of a man is the seeking after and the investigation of truth," Max added.

"But they didn't have a police force back in Cicero's day, did they?"

For the first time since they arrived, the detective smiled, showing his brilliant white teeth. When his face relaxed, he looked every bit as handsome as Liz remembered.

"I have to admit that this needs to be examined further." He scribbled a few more lines on his yellow pad.

"What are you going to do now?" Liz asked eagerly.

Wentworth raised his eyes from his notes and looked at her. He seemed to be having trouble keeping his face inscrutable but Liz couldn't tell whether the feeling he was trying to repress was amusement, excitement, or irritation.

"My job. And I suggest you go back to doing yours. We're making good progress on the case and you could jeopardize it by interfering."

He started to rise, as if to show them to the door.

"Before you send us packing, you might want to see the rest of the information we brought you," Max said.

"There's more? I gather business is very slow at your bookstore."

"Not really," Liz broke in, peeved by Wentworth's condescending attitude. "We just found out where Ste. Anne is, in case you're interested. It's in northern Ontario, not Quebec."

"I see," said Wentworth, looking a little puzzled.

Max looked puzzled too but he didn't resist as Liz took him by the arm and said, "Come on, Professor Bertrand. Let's not waste any more of the good detective's time." She practically dragged him out of the office.

"What's going on, Liz?" Max asked as soon as they were out on the street. "Why wouldn't you let me tell him about the fire? That's our biggest clue."

"He doesn't want our help and, frankly, I'm sick of being rejected by people," Liz said fiercely. "Let him figure it out on his own."

"But Liz ..." Max started.

"I can't handle any more negativity right now. Just drop it, okay?"

She waved down a passing cab saying she needed to get back to work and they rode to the bookstore in silence. Once her hand touched the doorknob she thought better of it. She couldn't face Georgia's curiosity. Not today. She clumped upstairs morosely, threw her purse onto a chair, pushed Jasper off the sofa, and lay down.

"Hi, Mum. What's up?" Josh came into the room, half a banana in his hand, half bulging in one cheek.

"Not me, that's for sure."

"I can see that." When his mother didn't laugh as anticipated, he came over and sat down beside her. "Are you still worried about Sammy?"

"More than anything else, although I seem to have more worries than I can handle these days."

He swallowed the rest of the banana and cleared his throat. "I feel really bad. This is my fault, isn't it?"

"You had good intentions, Joshie. When your sister gets over being mad, I'm sure she'll recognize that you were only worried about her because you love her."

"Except, if I'm really honest with myself, I have to admit that mostly I just didn't like Derek. He rubbed me the wrong way, so I wanted to prove that I was right about him, no matter whether or not it hurt Sammy," he said slowly. "I've been doing a lot of thinking, Mum, and I don't like what I've learned about myself."

"Join the club," Liz sighed.

LIZ GOT THROUGH THAT evening without calling Sammy by emptying her dresser drawers and sorting and refolding all her clothes. She made a pile of stuff to give to Goodwill: a couple of faded T-shirts, a beige cardigan Sammy had always hated on her, and a jacket with a hole she didn't know how to mend. Josh was happy to toss in two pairs of sweatpants that were too short in the legs, and a black and yellow striped knitted cap his granny had made that reminded him of a bumblebee. Then she spent a sleepless night prowling around the apartment looking for other things to purge: mostly useless souvenirs of her marriage, including a cookie jar from Adam's great aunt they had never used and a set of monogrammed towels she'd held onto for sentimental reasons.

Thursdays she was on her own at the bookstore so it was easy to keep occupied. After work she got her hair trimmed at the local salon and then took Josh out for gourmet hamburgers and sweet potato fries to keep them both out of the house as long as possible. Unable to sleep for the fourth night in a row, she snuck into Sammy's room and pulled *A Wrinkle in Time* off the bookshelf and read it curled up on her daughter's bed.

Friday morning, Georgia came into work. She was wonderfully objective about the whole situation, seeing it not as a crisis but simply a normal stage in the mother-daughter relationship, one bound to end in mutual respect and understanding. For a couple of hours after her assistant left Liz continued to feel hopeful, but by late afternoon she was panicking and by the evening — having resorted to Glenfiddich to keep her company, as Josh had gone straight from school to band practice and was going on from there to a party — she broke down and called Sammy on her cellphone.

There was no answer. Liz left a message, apologizing once again, begging her daughter to come home. Sammy did not call back. Liz took Jasper for a walk and then she sent her old roommate Melanie a long email about how she'd ruined her life.

Sammy returned her call around eight o'clock, very calm and brisk, saying she was sorry her mother was so upset but they needed some time apart. When Liz asked why four days wasn't enough time apart, Sammy replied that she was enjoying being with her father and getting to know his girlfriend. In fact, she admired Laura, who had inspired her to want to travel around the world and live in different places and do different things. Staying with her dad was useful practice in becoming more independent.

Liz bit her tongue, remembering what Georgia had said about this being a normal stage in their relationship. She said that she loved Sammy and missed her and hoped she'd come home soon. But she was furious at Laura, beautiful Laura, treacherous Laura who had gone behind her back and stolen her daughter. As soon as Sammy hung up, Liz started planning how to win that daughter back. She needed to do something to show that *she* could be daring and independent too. It wasn't just Sammy who had rejected her, both kids thought she was boring; Josh had said he she lived in a bubble. Well, she would show them that they were wrong. She wasn't as afraid of the real world as everyone thought. Laura and Adam might be going backpacking in Thailand, but she would do something equally dangerous. She would go to Northern Ontario and catch a killer.

Before she could change her mind, she called Max and asked if he was interested in taking a road trip. In his car, since she no longer owned one, her last vehicle having given out about the same time as her marriage. But she still had a licence and would be happy to do the driving. And to make sandwiches.

Max agreed to the plan. For the first time that week, Liz had a good night's sleep.

BY NINE A.M. THEY were on the road, despite warnings that it might snow. Max assured Liz that Environment Canada's predictions were usually wrong and that even if they proved to be correct, he had a lifetime of practice driving in winter conditions. They agreed that she would start out at the wheel so that he could take over if the weather got really bad.

Soon after Max requested they switch over from classical music to a jazz station they had to stop to refuel the car, then for half an hour traffic inched by a tractor-trailer that had jackknifed across two lanes of the highway and finally, just when a gathering storm was shredding Liz's nerves beyond reasonable tolerance, they changed drivers. Max drove the last hundred miles slowly and mostly in silence, squinting against the snowflakes that were flying into the high beams like kamikaze moths.

As the hours passed and the journey grew uncomfortable, the idea that the two of them could solve this — or any — crime appeared increasingly quixotic to Liz. Not that she regretted spending the day with Max. There was something about him that appealed to the part of herself she liked best; a kind of old-world courtliness that made her feel more feminine than she usually did. Or maybe it was just that she missed her father and Max missed his daughter. Whatever the reason, it was clear that he liked being with her as much as she liked being with him. She wondered if she had taken advantage of him by asking him to accompany her on this road to nowhere in order to address her own problems.

"I'm sorry I dragged you on this wild goose chase," she said.

"You didn't drag me anywhere, Liz. I've been the one pushing you into this investigation because for the first time since my wife died last year I'm actually excited about getting up in the morning."

"Tell me about your wife, Max."

"Tanya was Russian by birth, a musician by training, full of life right up to the end."

"What did she play?"

"The piano. She taught music at the conservatory and belonged to a jazz ensemble. Our home was always full of her colleagues and friends and students."

"It sounds like you miss her a lot."

"I do. I had to sell the house, even though Chantal begged me not to, because I couldn't bear to live there without Tanya."

"I envy you for having had such a great marriage."

"Was yours unhappy?" Max asked.

"No, I wouldn't say that. In fact, we're still pretty close. Especially in space, since Adam lives upstairs." She tried to sound nonchalant, but despite her best intentions, her tone was bitter.

"You don't have to talk about it if you don't want to, Liz. It's really none of my business."

"Yes it is, Max. You're my friend. I don't mind talking about it. It's just not very interesting. In a nutshell: Adam couldn't be faithful and I couldn't keep forgiving him."

"As my daughter often says, unconsciously borrowing a metaphor from Circe in Homer's *Odyssey*, men are such pigs."

"Except for you, darling Maxime. If only you were younger."

"You flatter me, my dear."

Just then the car in front of them stopped abruptly, its rear lights shining like panicked animal eyes through the swirling snow. Max jammed on the brakes, but despite having snow tires, his car went into a skid. He let up on the pedal and jerked the steering wheel to the right to avoid sliding into the other vehicle, or worse, into oncoming traffic. Their car spun around a full 360 degrees, Liz bracing herself against the glove compartment, waiting for the inevitable impact and the sound of shearing metal.

A voice she didn't recognize was shrieking. It was hers. Then it stopped and there was silence and a deep darkness all around them.

They sat, shaking, on the verge of the highway as other cars swerved by, horns blaring a pointless and belated warning. Max's knuckles on the steering wheel were as white as his face. Liz feared he was about to faint and silently twisted the cap off a bottle of water and offered it to him. He took a drink and then exhaled shakily.

"I think Tanya's spirit was protecting us. There's no other explanation for what just happened."

"Do you want me to take over? Or should we just turn around and go home?"

"No. There are only twenty kilometres more to go."

"I'm so so sorry, Max," Liz said. "All I wanted to do was earn my children's respect by doing something spontaneous and I almost got us killed."

"That was me at the wheel, in case you forgot," Max replied.

"It's not your fault the car in front of us stopped without warning. You just reacted instinctively."

"But I should have remembered to pump the brake gently, not jam it all the way down like that. Just keep navigating. I promise to drive more carefully from now on."

HALF AN HOUR LATER they pulled up outside the McKay residence, a small bungalow with grey siding like many others in its working-class neighbourhood. Some of the neighbours had built a second storey or added a garage, some had built picket fences or arbours or put up decorative shutters or lampposts; one even had a backyard pool complete with diving board. Brian McKay's place was unadorned, though in good repair. The hedge was trimmed, the path was freshly shovelled, and a large pile of firewood covered by a gray tarpaulin stood neatly stacked beside the front door.

Liz looked at Max. She couldn't quite believe what they were doing. "This is crazy, isn't it? I mean, what if he really is the killer? He might get violent."

"Not if we don't reveal our suspicions. Remember, we are just a little old man and a humble bookseller, bringing a man news of his foster brother's death. Just let me do the talking, Liz. I'm a very good liar."

"I've noticed that," said Liz, with a shaky laugh. Then she walked up to the door and knocked loudly, her heart beating a matching tattoo in her chest.

A tall, balding man opened the door, his face haggard and wary. She suddenly realized what an odd pair she and Max made: a middle-aged woman in a ski jacket and toque accompanied by a distinguished bearded gentleman in a cashmere coat, silk scarf, and beret. Doubtless the man at the door assumed that they were Jehovah's Witnesses or volunteers collecting money for a charitable foundation.

"Yes?"

"Hi," said Liz, her voice absurdly high. She cleared her throat, trying to sound like someone he would trust, someone calm and confident. "Are you Brian McKay?"

"Who wants to know?"

"My name is Elizabeth Ryerson and this is Professor Maxime

Bertrand. We drove here from Toronto to give you some unfortunate news."

"All the news that comes out of Toronto is unfortunate," he said wryly. "But if you drove such a long way in a blizzard just to talk to me, I guess I'd better invite you in."

He opened the door wider but did not offer to shake hands. They stood in the hall, awkwardly stamping the snow off their boots, until he said, "So, what's this all about?"

"Your foster brother, Andrew James Scott," said Max.

"Now, there's a name I haven't heard in a long time."

Rummaging around in the pocket of his faded flannel shirt, McKay pulled out a pack of Craven A cigarettes and lit one. Then he crossed to the living room and sat down heavily on a sofa covered in dark blue corduroy, tossing the spent match into an overflowing ashtray on the coffee table in front of it.

"What did he do now?" he asked, after filling and emptying his lungs with smoke.

"Nothing that we know of," said Max, stepping out of his boots and, without waiting for an invitation, sitting down on a shabbily upholstered armchair. The fabric was so worn that its blue and green plaid was almost invisible, but like the pale blue wall-to-wall carpet, it was very clean. A cream-coloured crocheted antimacassar covered the headrest. Probably the work of the late Mrs. McKay whose photograph, which Max recognized from the *Toronto Star* obituary, sat on one highly polished end table with a bunch of pink silk flowers in a crystal vase beside it. The television remote control and a TV guide sat on the other end table. There were few decorations in the room: a framed reproduction of Leonardo da Vinci's *Last Supper* hung over the fireplace, and a couple of family photographs — the McKays' wedding portrait, Brian's high school graduation picture — hung over the sofa.

McKay watched Max's silent scrutiny of the room with an unreadable expression on his face and then looked over at Liz, who was still standing in the hallway, and said dryly, "You might as well join the party."

She unzipped her boots and crossed the room to perch on an uncomfortable straight-backed chair whose back was covered with a multicoloured afghan. She worried that the man might ask them to leave at any moment. This interview was proving even more awkward than she had imagined it might be, but Max appeared unfazed.

"Mr. Scott was actually the victim," he continued.

"Victim?"

"Unfortunately, he was brutally murdered," Liz explained, watching for a reaction. The man's mouth twitched briefly but that was all.

"And I'm supposed to care?" This time the venom was unmistakable.

"Well, he was family, after all."

"For less than a year. Anyway, what's it to you?"

"I knew him," Liz said. At least that wasn't a complete lie. "And since you were his only surviving relative, I thought you would want to know what happened."

"He wasn't my blood relative, all right? Let's get that straight. And he destroyed my real family."

"You mean the fire?" said Liz.

"Yes, I mean the goddamn fire."

"He was terribly sorry," said Liz, with sudden conviction. After all, the man had spent his life in hiding. "He never got over it."

"Bullshit," McKay replied, meeting her gaze for the first time. His brown eyes were bloodshot, the skin around them prematurely wrinkled as though he spent a lot of time outdoors.

"Listen, my mother died in that fire. You knew that, right?" Those bloodshot eyes were suddenly full of tears, which he dashed away angrily with the back of his hand.

"Yes."

"So you want me to pretend that I'm shocked Scotty came to a bad end?" He put out his cigarette, which he'd smoked right down to the filter, then immediately lit a fresh one. "Get real."

"I'm sorry," said Liz sincerely. "I guess we came here for nothing."

"Let me explain something to you, lady. Andrew Scott wasn't always a city boy with an expensive car and nice suits. When he came to live with us he was a skinny little bastard who cringed every time you talked to him as though he expected to be hit. My God, it made you *want* to hit him! Anyhow, my mother rescued the poor bugger. And he thanked her by burning down our house with her still in it."

"It was a terrible tragedy," Max said. "Your feelings are very natural."

"Don't pretend to understand my feelings," McKay spat. "My grandfather built that house with his own two hands, but he thought insurance was a waste of money and so did my father. That's why we couldn't afford to rebuild it and had to rent this shit-box instead."

"It's a very nice place," Liz said politely.

McKay ignored her comment. "You'd think that Scotty would have wanted to help out when he got older and made some money. But no, he never sent us a goddamned penny. I'm amazed he told you that he was sorry for what he did, because he never told *us*!" Realizing that he was practically shouting, he took a deep breath and muttered, "Oh, forget it. What's the use?" and stood up abruptly.

They rose as well.

"I'm sorry to have brought back such painful memories, Mr. McKay," said Liz.

"I'm sure your intentions were good, but believe me, even though Scotty might have been your friend, he never was one to me. I wish to God he'd never come into my life."

They all shook hands solemnly and that was that.

HE FINALLY worked up the courage to ask Natalie out on a real date. It wasn't that he was afraid she'd reject him; women rarely rejected him and besides, she'd been saying for some time that it would be nice to spend more time together. What made him so nervous was that he wanted more than a casual date; he even wanted more than a passionate night followed by a hasty exit the following morning. He wanted Natalie herself.

He'd never allowed himself to feel this way about a woman before.

Until he met Natalie, it hadn't been a big effort to keep things light. The women he dated were often disappointed and some had been hurt, but since he'd always been a complete gentleman and let them initiate any intimacy that occurred, he'd been able to walk away from his romantic entanglements more or less guilt-free. But he couldn't imagine how he would do that this time.

He felt compelled to ask Natalie to dinner so he could sit opposite her over a snow-white tablecloth and sparkling crystal and watch her mouth as she talked. There was a little gap between her front teeth that any big-city girl would have had fixed in a minute, and a mole on her right cheek that looked just like black velvet. Her dark hair, usually pulled back in a businesslike ponytail, fell in loose waves around her shoulders, and her scoop-necked silk blouse revealed a chest full of freckles and collarbones as elegant as any ballerina's. She took a very long time deciding which roll to eat and once she chose the braided one, covered with poppy seeds, she cut it precisely in half and buttered both halves evenly before taking a single bite. He found this unaccountably moving.

"Tell me about yourself, James."

"There's not much to say."

"You always listen to me babbling on about my family, so now it's your turn to tell me about yours."

"I don't have any family that I'm aware of."

"You're an orphan?"

"My father ran off when I was a baby and my mother died a long time ago. I know she had a couple of brothers, but her family disowned her for getting pregnant and dropping out of high school so I've never actually met any of them."

"No wonder you always seem so sad."

He was shocked. Nobody had ever suggested that he seemed

sad. Aloof maybe; he'd been called that a few times. Standoffish, even conceited, but never sad.

"Do I really seem sad to you, Natalie?"

"Oh yes. Especially when I talk about my brothers and sisters. You get this look on your face ... well, now I understand why. But I have an idea."

"What's that?"

"We should find them. Your family, I mean. We do that kind of stuff all the time at my office, for the disposition of wills, and tracking down deadbeat dads, and so on. You'd be surprised how easy it is."

"What makes you think they'd want to hear from me?" he said, putting down his wineglass abruptly. It spilled. He dabbed at the spreading red stain with his napkin to cover up his discomfort. The idea of meeting the people who abandoned his mother made him feel sick to his stomach.

"Who knows? They might be nice, James. You might have lots of cousins. You might even have grandparents wishing they knew where you were. It's worth a try."

Their food arrived, which was a good distraction. As usual, he'd ordered a steak and a baked potato, while she'd asked for the bouillabaisse, a word he couldn't pronounce. He'd recently moved into a new condo with a state-of-the-art chef's kitchen: stainless steel Sub-Zero fridge, double oven and separate thirty-inch gas-fired cooktop, and an integrated wine cooler and bar sink on the black-granite-topped island. It was easy enough to get her to talk about what kind of pots and pans he still needed to buy if he really wanted to become a gourmet cook, and what her favourite recipes were. But eventually she returned, more tentatively this time, to the topic of finding his family.

"Look, James, I'm sorry for being pushy before. There's absolutely no reason you should go looking for people you've never met. I just thought it might give you some comfort to find out you weren't all alone in the world."

"But don't you think we really are alone, Natalie?" he asked, genuinely curious.

"No, I don't. Not if we have family who loves us. My own family would do anything for me."

"Well, you're lucky."

"I'm not the only one. I know other families who have gone through hell and come back together stronger for it."

"For example?"

"For example, my best friend back home was in a terrible car accident at the end of senior year. She'd been drinking. We all had. We'd built a bonfire on the beach and had a lot of beers. So she should never have been behind the wheel in the first place." Natalie sighed. "Long story short, her little brother died in the crash."

"That's terrible."

"It was. He wasn't even supposed to be there because he was two years younger than us. But he begged and begged to come to the party with the graduating class and Camille could never say no to him. Afterwards she felt so guilty that she didn't want to live anymore, so she took a whole bottle of Tylenol. Luckily, her father found her in time to get her stomach pumped."

"What happened then?"

"Life went on. We had to convince her that what she did was stupid and irresponsible but not wicked, you know? It took a long time, but she was able to forgive herself. After all, even her parents forgave her."

He sat in a daze, taking in what Natalie had said to him. Why had she told him this story? It was almost as if she knew.

"Her parents forgave her?" He couldn't imagine such a thing.

"Yes. She's married now and has a little boy named Gaétan after her brother. Her mother takes care of him during the day so she can go to work."

"They sound like amazing people."

"They're ordinary people, James. Just like you and me."

"You don't know me, Natalie." He blinked back the tears that had begun to fill his eyes. Maybe he could say that there was something in his contact lens and escape to the bathroom?

"But I want to know you, James. I like you."

"I like you too. I like you a lot. It's just that I did some really bad stuff when I was younger and I'm afraid you wouldn't want to be my friend anymore if you knew about it."

"Try me."

"Not tonight, Natalie. But maybe one day."

"Soon." She reached over and took his hand.

"Okay, soon."

13

THE STORM HAD SPENT itself while Max and Liz were inside. Snow covered the branches of an enormous blue spruce. It lay in silent glittering mounds in all the yards and on all the rooftops around them. Away from the sulphurous glare of the city the sky was huge; a bright silver moon hung low in the sky and stars in their thousands danced overhead. As they stood, admiring the dazzling expanse above them, the tumult of emotions they had just experienced became insignificant; even delusional. No merely human drama was important in the face of the unknowable cosmos.

Liz switched on the ignition, hoping to get some heat, though she wasn't ready to drive away quite yet. She felt very dissatisfied with the way things had gone. Could this interview with a lost soul be the big confrontation she had risked her life — and Max's — for? Had they really accomplished anything more than disturbing an already disturbed person?

She'd asked so few of the questions that still haunted her. Why had Andrew James Scott been put into foster care? What happened to his birth family? Why did Scott burn down the McKay house? Did the McKay family press charges and were there any criminal proceedings? Where did Scott go afterwards? There were seventeen years of missing history to fill in between the fire in Ste. Anne in October 1989 and the murder in Toronto in October 2006.

And on the tip of her tongue, unspoken, were the most important questions of all, the ones she'd been afraid to ask because they would reveal that she had been snooping. Why had Brian McKay been looking for James Scott? And had he found him?

"What do you think, Max?" she asked. "Did the man we just met murder James Scott?"

"I don't think we have enough to go on yet, Liz. Obviously, Brian McKay had good reason to hate his foster brother. Obviously, he's a lonely man. But a murderer? I'm not sure. He seems too beaten down to be violent, frankly."

"But didn't you find it odd that when I said that Scott had been 'brutally murdered' he didn't react at all? Didn't ask how, or when, or any of the other questions a normal person would ask?"

"That was a bit suspicious."

"And he knew that Scott had become a city boy with nice suits and a fancy car, which suggests that he saw him recently."

"That was even more suspicious," Max conceded. "Although I suppose a lawyer could argue that he simply deduced those facts, since you said you were Scott's friend and you came from the big city ..."

"And there was something else," Liz said slowly. "Did you see how incredibly clean his house was?"

"Especially in contrast to this car," Max laughed, his feet rustling in paper bags and Styrofoam coffee cups, the wreckage of the food they'd consumed on the way up.

"Everything was spotless and shining except for that ashtray," Liz continued. "Either he never empties it, which would be out of character, or he's been sitting there chain-smoking all day. Which means the man is stressed out about something."

"You are a natural-born detective, Elizabeth Ryerson," Max smiled. "Luckily for both of us, my talents lie in another direction. Last night after you called me proposing this expedition, I made dinner reservations at a lovely inn. And after we enjoy the prix fixe menu we shall discover whether their pillow-top mattresses are as comfortable as advertised. After all, we need a good night's sleep before our long drive home tomorrow."

THE INN WAS AS charming as Max had indicated and the cuisine was exceptional, relying heavily on local fish and game. They both had the pumpkin and apple soup to start, but Max opted for venison stew while Liz chose the smoked whitefish risotto. Despite working their way through the bread basket and an entire bottle of Riesling — Max insisted that it would work equally well with fish or game and since Liz had no opinion about wine except that she liked to drink it, she was happy to let him select whatever he wanted — they managed to share a portion of dark-chocolate-and-orange cake for dessert. Liz couldn't remember the last time she had eaten such elegant food or felt so far away from her everyday life. The waiter assumed that they were a father and daughter travelling together. She didn't bother to correct him. Everything that had happened so far that day had felt unreal, so she decided to stop thinking and just go along with the fantasy.

Max had reserved adjoining rooms, refusing to let her pay a penny. Hers had a four-poster bed made up prettily with a thick eiderdown and masses of pillows. But for the fact that she was exhausted, she thought it would be a shame to disturb its symmetry by sleeping in it. She had a long bath in the deep vintage tub and then read most of a two-year-old issue of *The New Yorker* from a tidy stack beside the bed. Despite the long drive, the near-accident, and her suspicion that Brian McKay was indeed guilty of his foster brother's murder, this had been the best day Liz could remember having for a very long time.

Breakfast was as good as dinner and they took their time enjoying the homemade blueberry jam and scones and coffee with steamed milk, but they eventually had to heave themselves up from the table to get back on the road. The drive home, though long, was uneventful; the most exciting thing that happened was their sighting of a pair of deer beside the highway. Once they finally reached the eighteen lanes of horror on the 401 into Toronto — where truck drivers amused themselves tailgating family sedans and young men changed lanes at 130 kilometres an hour, giving the finger to anyone who objected — they longed for the calm of the country roads they had just left. Liz was grateful that she rarely had a reason to drive, especially when she unfolded herself from the car seat and discovered she could barely climb up the stairs to her apartment, her hips were so stiff.

Instead of boasting to her children about this daring adventure in order to earn earn their admiration, she reluctantly decided to tell them nothing about it, at least for now. After all, what could she say? "Max and I interviewed a murder suspect but he wouldn't confess"? It made more sense to keep quiet until after consulting with Detective Wentworth, as much as she was dreading that interview. If the police acted on the information she and Max had garnered, she would be able to tell the kids how her fearlessness and cunning helped crack the case.

If not, they would be spared yet another reason to be disappointed in her.

Before leaving, she had told her family that Max needed to make the trip and she was going along just to keep him company, and she stuck with that story. Josh was delighted with the can of maple syrup she brought back as a souvenir and immediately asked if they could have French toast for supper; otherwise, he was completely uninterested in where she'd been or what she'd been doing. Jasper seemed to be the only one who suspected that something strange was going on, greeting her with less enthusiasm than usual and whimpering a bit for no obvious reason. He was probably just picking up on her nervousness about the task ahead: explaining to Detective Wentworth that not only had she not abandoned the investigation as he'd requested, she'd also secretly confronted a possible murderer.

MONDAY MORNING, LIZ AND Max headed off to the police station full of adrenalin and resolve only to discover that Detective Wentworth wasn't there. Liz wanted to come back later; she didn't want to speak to anybody but Detective Wentworth because he was yet another person who had made her feel inadequate. She wanted to see his face when he realized that she was smarter — and braver — than he thought she was. If nothing else, it would be a trial run for telling her children the true purpose of her trip up north.

But Max didn't want to come back later. He was convinced that it was crucial to get things moving as quickly as possible, and persuaded her that they should leave the detective a note. All they needed to say was that, as a child, Andrew James Scott had set the fire that killed Brian McKay's mother, and let the police take it from there. After all, he and Liz didn't have any conclusive evidence to offer, did they? No murder weapon covered with fingerprints, no confession. Why should they let Wentworth know that they had confronted Brian McKay in person? He was bound to be furious, and his anger with them might distract him from pursuing the case properly.

Liz was disappointed that their investigation had such an anticlimactic conclusion but there didn't seem to be any more avenues to pursue. They left Wentworth a note and went home.

WHEN THE DETECTIVE RETURNED to his office from breaking up a domestic dispute and found it, he was caught between anger and admiration. Somehow these two complete amateurs, a dandified old academic and a charmingly ditzy bookseller, kept digging up clues that his team missed. It was maddening. But he was damned if he was going to let pride stand in the way of catching a killer, so he forced himself to follow their lead right away.

It wasn't hard to get confirmation that indeed, arson had been blamed for Mrs. McKay's death and that her foster son had confessed to the crime. Andrew James Scott must have been in juvenile detention afterwards, which explained why there was no record of his whereabouts for so many years, but Wentworth thought he could get those records unsealed if he had to, given that Scott himself was no longer alive.

Meanwhile, he was more interested in investigating Brian McKay, so he got permission to search the man's phone records. It didn't take long to discover that, a month after McKay had run that ad on Craigslist, he'd made a few calls to one particular youth custody centre up north. The staff at the facility, protective of all their charges, refused to speak to Wentworth until Division verified his identity and reminded them that he was pursuing a homicide investigation. Then he had to play telephone tag with several more close-mouthed people before locating a social worker who acknowledged having met Brian McKay when he visited in August.

"We're not supposed to give out any information about former residents, but Mr. McKay was so distraught," she said. "He needed to find his brother because their father had just died and he wanted to invite him to the funeral."

"Were you able to give him any information?" Wentworth asked, not bothering to point out that McKay Senior's funeral had taken place in July. The woman sounded upset enough already.

"Not really. It had been too many years since the boy left here."

"You said 'not really,'" Wentworth pointed out. "Not 'no.' Does that mean you were able to tell Brian McKay something, however vague, about the whereabouts of Andrew James Scott?"

"I felt sorry for him," she admitted reluctantly. "I had recently lost my mother so when he started to cry, I ended up crying too. I understood exactly how he was feeling. He seemed so … lost. Reaching out for comfort. You know."

Wentworth waited for her to finish blowing her nose and then asked, "What did you do then?"

"I got the boy's file, and saw that he had taken the bus to Toronto when he left here, back in 1995."

"Was that all the information you gave to Brian McKay?" Wentworth was persistent, because he could tell from the woman's voice that she was still holding something back.

"I also gave him a contact in Toronto," she confessed.

"Who was that?"

"A former resident from the same period. A man who'd become very successful and is now one of our biggest private donors. I thought he might have some idea where Andrew Scott went."

"I need that number too, ma'am. Right away. I'll hold while you find it."

The contact in Toronto confirmed that Brian McKay had left several messages at his office but he hadn't responded until September because he had been on holiday in Europe with his wife. Anyway, the only thing he'd been able to tell McKay was that Andrew Scott — the boy everyone called "Ghost" because he was so pale — had talked a lot about wanting to go into the real estate business one day.

"I felt sorry I couldn't really help the guy more. Because Ghost always seemed like such a lonely kid. He was an orphan, eh? So when we were in juvie no one came to visit him, no one wrote him a letter or sent him a birthday card. It was really sad. And he was the only kid I ever heard of who stayed there longer than he had to, because he had nowhere else to go.

"After he got out he was still kind of shy. So naturally, I thought it would be great if he discovered he still had family who cared about him. Because that's what saved me, you know. Family."

TUESDAY MORNING, WENTWORTH CALLED the police in Ste. Anne to tell them he would be faxing them information about the case he was working on, and asking them to find out everything they could about his principal suspect. It didn't take them long to call back.

"Brian McKay was an only child. Maybe that's why his folks decided to take in a foster child in the first place. McKay Senior outlived his wife by seventeen years; he just died this past summer of a heart attack. Junior was living with him at the time."

"He never left home?"

"He did, but he came back. After high school he got a welder's licence. He had a pretty good job with a building contractor in Sault Ste. Marie for a few years. But he didn't stay there. These days, he's working at the saw mill in Ste. Anne."

"Is he clean?"

"Except for a couple of DUIs. The last one was right after his father's funeral. That little incident gave us the information you wanted about his vehicle. It's a black 1996 Ford F-150, the same size and weight as the truck that left tire tracks at your crime scene."

"Can you go to his place with a warrant and check the tires to see if they match too?" He couldn't believe it. The case was virtually solved.

"We're on our way."

WHEN THE LOCAL POLICE arrived at the McKay residence, a black Ford pickup was parked beside the house as though waiting for them. As they expected, the tires were a match to those that had left imprints at the crime scene but, oddly enough, there were no tracks on the pristine white driveway. In fact, the truck didn't look like it had been moved for a couple of days. The windshield was thick with ice and three inches of snow sat on the roof of the vehicle.

Not a good sign.

As soon as they opened the door and the smell hit them, they knew what they would find: Brian McKay upstairs in bed, in freshly ironed blue cotton pyjamas, an empty bottle of Xanax and a half-empty fifth of Crown Royal on the night table beside him. There was also a neatly typed letter.

Sunday, November 12, 2006

Andrew Scott killed my mother. I killed Andrew Scott. That's perfect justice, isn't it? Except I didn't realize that he'd told anybody about setting fire to my house and killing my mother, but some old French guy and a blond lady from Toronto tracked me down and they knew everything. There's no way I'm waiting for the police to show up next. So I guess he gets the last laugh after all.

I knew he was rotten from the day we met. What kind of kid gets rejected by his own mother? Of course, my mother said it wasn't his fault. But she was always too trusting. After all, look what happened to her!

What happened to him? A few years in juvie, that's all. A normal person would have felt guilty and sent us some money or something, especially once he got rich. But Scotty never gave us a damn thing.

Because of Andrew Scott I don't have much to leave my cousin Cameron McKay over in Blind River, even though he and Jeanie were always good to my father and me. They can clear out my savings account and take whatever they want from this house and give the rest to charity. I bought the sofa last year, it's in decent shape, but everything else is crap. Unless that tray in the dining room is real silver like Mom claimed but I don't think it is.

Here's the driver's licence and registration and insurance
for my truck. The rent here is paid up until April 1st. I don't
owe anybody anything.

Brian McKay

THE OFFICER AT THE front desk pushed some buttons and
spoke briefly into an intercom, and soon Liz and Max were
being shown to Detective Wentworth's office once again. It was
Friday afternoon. Presumably he had made some progress on
the case since they left him their note Monday morning. And
yet he barely acknowledged their presence, continuing to talk
on the phone while waving at them to sit down. They waited
uncomfortably as he grunted "Yes," "Okay," "That makes sense,"
and "Just do it" to the person on the other end of the line.
When he finally hung up, he mumbled, "Sorry, I have to type
this report while it's still clear in my head." They had to sit for
another five minutes, wondering why he'd sent for them. Liz
kept having flashbacks of being called into the principal's office
for some high school misdemeanour.

Finally, Wentworth looked up from his computer and said,
"So, you two. I asked you here to inform you that the investigation into the death of Andrew James Scott is now officially
closed, although not in the way we would have preferred."

"What happened?" asked Liz.

"On Sunday, November 21st, Brian McKay left a suicide note
confessing to the murder."

Liz gasped. "A suicide note? You mean, he killed himself?"

There was a stab in her own chest as she said this, as though guilt had prongs. Had she caused the man's death by hunting him down?

Wentworth didn't reply. He simply pushed the note, encased in a clear plastic sleeve, across the table. Liz and Max read it silently.

"This is my fault, isn't it?" said Liz, starting to cry.

"You never know what can happen when you get involved in a criminal investigation. That's why I warned you to keep out of it, Ms. Ryerson."

"But you would have found McKay eventually without our help, wouldn't you?" said Max, indignantly.

"For sure," Wentworth conceded. "We already had a good description of him from the staff of a restaurant he and Scott had dinner at on the night of the murder. We even knew the man's name was Brian. Once we had figured out who this 'Brian' was in relation to Scott, we would have been able to match the tires on his truck to the tracks found at the scene. You just sped things up."

"Then why are you trying to make Liz feel responsible for his death?"

"I never suggested that she was responsible for his death. Nonetheless, her involvement in this case — and yours too, I might add — was completely inappropriate, and I cannot condone it."

"Obviously you have to take the official line. I appreciate that," said Max.

In spite of himself, Wentworth smiled. "Was there anything else?"

"Oh yes," Max replied. "I have all kinds of unanswered questions. For example, why do you think Mr. McKay waited so long to take his revenge? And why did he kill Mr. Scott in Wychwood Park? And how did he kill him?"

"Sorry to disappoint you, but although TV shows make it seem like successful police investigations tie everything up in a big red bow, half the time crucial information remains missing and we just have to be satisfied with getting dangerous people off the street."

"Well, surely you know quite a bit more than you've told us," Max persisted.

"Not really. As to how James Scott died, we know he was killed by a blow to the head, but we never found the murder weapon. As to why he died in Wychwood Park, he and McKay exchanged angry words in a restaurant near there half an hour before his estimated time of death, but nobody could tell us the subject of their argument or why they left the place without eating. And we'll also never know why Brian McKay waited so long, or what exactly set him off. Although that cousin he mentioned in his suicide note told the police McKay had been troubled for years."

Liz was afraid that if she opened her mouth nothing would come out but a howl. She had been convinced that solving Scott's murder would help the world make sense again. Instead, it just made things worse.

"Obviously he was troubled, since he committed suicide," Max observed. "But as Seneca once wrote, 'every guilty person is his own hangman.'"

"If that were true, the police would be out of a job," Wentworth laughed, breaking some of the tension in the room.

Then he turned to Liz, who was still sobbing into a crumpled Kleenex. "Look, Ms. Ryerson, I'm sorry if I was hard on you before, but I was pretty upset when I found out you two confronted Brian McKay. He was a desperate man. He could have killed you instead of himself."

"I don't think he would have," she sniffled. "He was just terribly, terribly sad, and frustrated with his life. He didn't threaten us. All his anger was focused on James Scott, on how he had never paid the family back for what they'd lost."

"But you couldn't have known that before you met him, could you?" Wentworth continued.

"No, I guess not."

"Sometimes even sad and lonely people are driven to acts of violence when they feel cornered. You're just lucky he took it out on himself instead of on you."

"I don't feel lucky," Liz whispered.

"I understand. So take my advice. If you and the professor ever feel like dabbling in crime again, I suggest you read about how Oedipus killed his father and Clytemnestra killed her husband. Leave the real-life blood and gore to us professionals, all right?"

"THAT DETECTIVE WENTWORTH IS quite an impressive fellow," said Max in the cab on the way back to the bookstore. "Smart, articulate, and well-read. I can see why you like him."

"What makes you think I like him? He thinks I'm an idiot," said Liz, sniffling. "And he's right. If I hadn't insisted on snooping, maybe that poor man would still be alive."

"That's simply not true. Whether Brian McKay killed himself out of guilt about the crime he committed or fear of the consequences of that crime, the outcome would have been the same."

"But why was I meddling in other people's business in the first place? I can't figure out my *own* life, Max. Everything is such a mess."

"Dear Elizabeth, you've just been going through a rough patch."

"That's one way of putting it. Sammy hates me. She's been living upstairs at Adam's for more than a week now. And since Adam wants to sell the building so he can live happily ever after with Laura, Josh will have to move in with him too, because I'll lose my business and become a bag lady, wandering around the streets with all my worldly goods in a shopping cart, sharing park benches with pigeons."

"Hmmm," Max said thoughtfully. "Maybe that's one problem I can actually help you with."

"What do you mean?"

"Well, much as it will disappoint the indefatigable Ms. Horvath, it appears I will not be buying a house in Hillcrest Village after all. However, I might consider investing in a bookstore instead …"

"Max, that's totally crazy!"

"No crazier than playing detective. To be frank, running a bookstore has been a fantasy of mine for a very long time. And our recent adventures have reminded me how much happier I am when I'm working. I need to keep busy, Liz."

Liz gave in to tears again. She had run out of tissues and

was forced to wipe her nose on her sleeve. "I don't know what to say, except thank you. But I won't hold you to this ridiculously generous offer once you realize what a mistake it is.

"And now I'm getting out of this cab before I embarrass both of us, and our poor driver, any further."

THOUGH HER EYES WERE so swollen from crying she could hardly see where she was going, Liz let Jasper lead her back to the pond at Wychwood Park, where she stood for some time, too dazed to move. Her thoughts were simultaneously hectic and monotonous, like a concerto by Vivaldi. She couldn't let Max rescue her just because he felt sorry for her. It was gallant of him to pretend his offer was motivated by self-interest rather than generosity, but she knew better. And anyway, she deserved to suffer. She had made a mess of this investigation the same way she'd made a mess of things with Sammy. All she had wanted to know was why James Scott was killed in Wychwood Park — and that was exactly what she had failed to find out. Instead, her interference had caused another man's death.

If she'd only minded her own business, none of this would have happened. Or at least that was what Detective Wentworth had implied. On the other hand, Maxime was convinced McKay would have committed suicide anyway. Was that really possible? Or was he just trying, as usual, to make her feel better? Brian McKay was obviously unbalanced, but losing his mother that way was enough to make anybody unbalanced. So maybe he wasn't criminally responsible for killing James Scott. He'd probably been suffering from PTSD or something like that.

Still, James Scott had suffered too. After all, he had only been a child at the time of the fire, and a foster child at that. Besides which, he'd paid for his crime in juvenile detention. So no matter how much Brian McKay resented him, he had no right to kill Scott. And anyway, she didn't believe in capital punishment; what was *wrong* with her, trying to decide who did or did not have the right to kill someone else? And why did Wentworth's disapproval bother her so much? The case was solved and she'd never see him again. He could go on feeling superior in the privacy of his stuffy office if it made him happy; it was nothing to do with her. He could scribble *Case Closed* across the cover of a file like they did on television and that would be the end of it.

She turned away from the pond.

"It seems like I'm on a steady diet of humble pie these days, Jasper," she said to the dog, who wagged his tail enthusiastically in response. It was possible he recognized the word *pie*, but most likely he was just happy that she was leaving the place where bad things happened.

"I know what you're thinking. If you can eat the same brand of kibble day after day, I should be able to get used to the taste of humble pie. Right, boy?"

The idea of pie inspired Liz to make a quiche for supper. It would only be her and Josh tonight, but she had become so accustomed to vegetarian cuisine that she couldn't bring herself to cook meat anymore, even when Sammy wasn't around. The telltale smell would linger for a long time afterwards and she didn't want her skittish daughter to find another reason not to come home. Besides, she'd lost her taste for animal flesh, what with Jasper being the only creature who still loved her unreservedly; the only creature she hadn't let down in some way.

When Josh came home, Liz was up to her elbows in flour, rolling out the pie crust with considerably more muscle than required because it felt therapeutic. Maybe she should go to chef school, where she could learn to wield some really heavy weapons. Lethally sharp knives. Mallets. Skewers.

"Dessert?" her son asked. He looked a lot like Jasper at that moment, wide-eyed and eager.

"No. A quiche for supper."

"Can you put spinach and cheese in it?"

"Sure. If you run over to Mr. Kim's and get me a package of frozen spinach."

"I don't really feel like going out again. Just cheese is good enough."

"What's wrong, Joshie?" He was slumped over on a kitchen chair, his head buried in Jasper's fur.

"It was a long day."

"What happened?"

"I decided I should give Derek another chance, so I took him out for lunch. We went for sushi. It cost me a fortune."

"I'm proud of you. That was very mature."

"I know, right? Sometimes I surprise myself." He laughed. "Anyhow, he's had kind of a tough life. He has two younger sisters and one does gymnastics and the other takes piano lessons and both of them need braces, and his mother's been trying to raise them all on a waitress's salary. No child support from the dad, he totally skipped out on the family. So Derek made some stupid mistakes, mostly when he was trying to make money to help his mother, but I think he's learned his lesson and now he's legit."

"Really?" Was she supposed to admire Derek now?

"Yeah. Actually, I really wish I'd got to know him better before I brought all that shit down on Sammy."

"I wish you had too. It would have saved us all a lot of trouble."

"I'm sorry, Mum."

"I'm not the one you need to apologize to, Josh. You need to talk to your sister."

"Can you come with me?"

"No." Liz was surprised by the firmness with which she replied.

"Please, Mum? I'm afraid of her."

"I know. I'm afraid of her, too. But she and I have our own stuff to work out with each other, and I have to save my strength for that. You can call me in for support if you need me, but honestly, I don't think you will."

14

A COUPLE OF HOURS LATER Josh came back downstairs to
grab his coat.

"I'm taking Sammy out for coffee at the Gâteau Basque."

"She's talking to you again?"

"Yeah."

"I'm so happy! Do you have enough money?"

"Well, given how much I already spent on Derek today ..."

"Here. Get yourself a *pain au chocolat* as well."

"Thanks, Mum. Will do. I'll try to persuade Sammy to eat
something too."

THE NEXT DAY, LIZ buried herself in her least favourite work, paying bills, as a way of punishing herself for messing up her life while simultaneously forcing every other thought from her mind. The manoeuvre was working pretty well. If she devoted this much attention to managing her business from now on, she'd do a lot better financially. And if Max was really going to become her partner, she was determined to make sure he didn't regret his decision.

She hadn't told anyone about his offer yet — not Adam, not even Georgia — in case it was just a fleeting impulse prompted by his desire to cheer her up, but she couldn't help hoping he would follow through on it. Thinking about the possibility started a flutter of joy in her chest, like a spangled butterfly winging through a gloomy cave. Despite her decision to impress her children by doing new things and going new places, she wasn't ready to give up her shop. Liz really loved selling books; it was what she was meant to do. She should try to become more successful at what she was doing instead of settling for subsistence living. She could even expand into the antiquarian book business on the Internet. Some people seemed to be doing very well at it and there didn't seem to be a great deal of risk involved.

Alternatively, she could sign up for cooking classes or go camping in the wilderness or take up running marathons or travel somewhere exotic. She could try to become a more interesting person. She *needed* to become a more interesting person. Once she had considered going on a photography safari in Africa. Surely that was still a worthwhile goal. Of course, Adam had always been the photographer, not her, so maybe that was a borrowed fantasy.

Liz sighed. It would take a lot of excavation to discover the person she was under all the incremental layers of marriage and motherhood, if there really was such a person. Maybe she had morphed so much through all these years of accommodating others that that wasn't possible anymore.

The phone rang and she picked it up distractedly, still thinking about what might lie ahead for her.

"Outside of a Dog Rare and Used Books. Liz Ryerson speaking."

"Hi, Ms. Ryerson. Keith Wentworth here."

"Detective," she answered, trying to keep the dread out of her voice. "I thought you said the case was closed. Unless you have new information?"

"No, no. This isn't police business. I'm actually calling about your area of expertise."

"How can I help you?" She was baffled.

"I'm looking for Christmas presents. My mother collects old books about Toronto and I thought maybe you would have some at your store."

"Fiction or non-fiction?"

"Non-fiction. Preferably with lots of period photographs."

"We have quite a few."

"Great. I'll see you in about an hour."

When Wentworth arrived, Liz asked Georgia if she could take care of other customers for a few minutes.

"Hey Lizzie, he's cute!" Georgia whispered, raising one pierced eyebrow.

"He's a policeman," Liz replied curtly, beckoning the detective to follow her to the kitchenette in the back of the store, where she had spread out the Toronto books on the table.

"Here's everything we have in stock," she said.

Wentworth took a list from his pocket and checked it against the titles on the table.

"I'll take the one on the islands. She has all the others."

"How long has your mother been collecting books about Toronto?"

"Since we moved here from Jamaica, back in 1978."

"I thought I detected a Caribbean accent. It's faint, but it's still there."

"You should hear me when I go home to visit my grandmother," he laughed.

"According to my kids, I revert to an English accent whenever I talk to my mother on the phone, and I moved to Canada ten years before you did. It never really goes away, does it?"

"It just goes underground," he nodded.

"What brought your family to Toronto? Work?"

"Not exactly. My dad used to run a limousine service back in Jamaica. He also made good money as a tour guide because there wasn't anything he didn't know about the island. But crime was getting bad there, so he decided to move somewhere my sister and I could grow up in safety."

"It seems kind of ironic that you became a cop, then," said Liz. Then she blushed. "I'm really sorry, Detective Wentworth; that was a stupid thing to say."

"First of all, call me Keith, and, secondly, you're right. But my dad never got to see the irony."

"What do you mean? And please, call me Liz."

"At first, moving to Canada seemed like it had been a good decision. Mum was a teacher so she got a job right away and made lots of new friends, and Dad worked as a taxi driver, which he enjoyed. He was a great raconteur, a real people-person, so there was nothing he liked better than picking up strangers all day long and talking to them. And although I didn't do as well academically as my sister, Iris — she's a dentist now — I managed to get into law school."

"You're a lawyer?"

"No, I dropped out."

"Why?"

"When I was in second year, my dad was killed by a late-night fare. A crackhead who stole all his money."

"I'm so, so sorry." Liz couldn't believe it. James Scott was the only murder victim she had ever met, but this man's own father had been murdered, and now he had to deal with violent death all the time. How could he maintain his composure? Or his sanity?

"Yeah, it was awful. My mother never got over it. In some ways, I'm not sure I have either."

Well, apparently that composure was just on the surface. He felt more than he showed. "What do you mean?" she asked.

"My whole life changed after that. At first I was so angry at my father's killer I wanted to gouge his eyes out with my thumbs. Then when I actually saw him in court, a twitching wreck of a man with sores all over his face and rotten teeth, sobbing that it was an accident, that my father shouldn't have tried to grab the gun, I got angry at my father instead for having been so bloody stupid."

Now Liz understood why this man had been angry at her! If she'd been shot by Brian McKay, her own children would have gone through exactly what he had. She didn't know what to say.

"But eventually I realized that I was just like Dad, a bright boy who counted too much on charm to get by. I quit law school because I didn't want to hang around with other kids like me anymore. Besides which, theoretical discussions of jurisprudence no longer engaged me. All I wanted to do was stop bad things from happening. By the time they got to court, it was already too late."

"So, do you find police work satisfying?" she asked, genuinely curious.

"Yes and no," he said. "When we solve crimes and catch the bad guys, sure, it's satisfying. But not all crimes have easy solutions and not all bad guys turn out to be unambiguously bad. As you saw with the Scott murder."

"Life is so messy! That's why I've always preferred books," Liz said ruefully, and they grinned at each other. She had forgotten how much she liked Detective Wentworth's smile.

"Speaking of which, how about helping me find a Christmas present for a four-year-old girl obsessed with *The Lion King*?"

"Your daughter?" Liz asked, trying to hide her disappointment.

"No, I'm not married. It's for my partner's little girl, Sarah."

SAMMY WAS STILL AVOIDING her mother, leaving early for school and coming home while Liz was at work. They occasionally chatted awkwardly on the stairs because she refused to enter the flat. Liz called on the phone a few times with reminders about dentist appointments and other incidentals but she didn't want to be too intrusive, hoping that eventually Sammy would be willing to come home on her own.

And, if she were totally honest with herself, Liz would have to admit that her daughter's absence had freed up a little space that allowed occasional thoughts of Keith Wentworth to creep in. It would have been more difficult to give herself permission to fantasize about any man — much less someone five years younger — if Sammy had been around with her X-ray vision. But, because Josh was more oblivious to the nuances of her moods than Sammy, she could negotiate some privacy when she had only her son to deal with. She could even go out on a date and not worry about being interrogated afterwards.

Shortly after his visit to the bookstore, Wentworth called Liz to ask how she was recovering from her brush with homicide.

"Better, thanks."

"Things going well at work?"

"Yes, this is our busiest time of year, which is good. It keeps me from brooding too much about finding the late James Scott and then meeting his brother, Brian."

"You know what you need, Liz Ryerson? You need to go out and have some fun. Some real distraction."

"I don't do 'fun,'" Liz replied, dubiously. "At least, not the kind of things that most people call fun. Team sports, for example, or amusement parks, or pub crawls or — God forbid — karaoke. I prefer to go to bed early with a good book."

"Not tonight," he insisted. "Tonight you're going to play pool."

"Pool? As in poking balls with a stick?"

"Something like that," he laughed. "Come on, I know a great place with antique pool tables and gourmet food. You'll like it, I promise. It's quirky and old-fashioned, kind of like you."

Liz was astonished. She couldn't think of a good reason to refuse. She spent that evening laughing so hard she could barely steady her cue. Wentworth, whom she wasn't able to think of as "Keith" yet, leaned over her a couple of times to demonstrate the proper stance, but otherwise didn't make a single move that could be interpreted as flirtatious. She didn't know whether to be relieved or regretful, but meanwhile she was indeed having a lot of fun.

"I've always been hopeless at sports," she said. "But at least with this one I don't have to coordinate my arms and legs at the same time, or worry about running into somebody else and knocking them down."

"That's lesson two, next week. We're working up to it," he said.

"I'M SURE I HEARD a strange man's voice down here the other night," said Adam, who had come by with a detailed itinerary of his trip complete with phone numbers and emergency contacts. "Is something going on that I should know about?"

"He's just a friend," Liz replied. "We went out to shoot some pool."

"I'm glad to hear that you're socializing more, Lizzie."

"You are?"

"Definitely. You're alone far too much. That's why you blow stuff out of proportion, like that weird detective thing you got into, or your freak-out over Sammy's relationship with Derek."

"Well, thank you, Sigmund Freud."

"I really wasn't trying to dump on you, Liz. I know it's hard for you to accept, but I want you to be happy."

"You know what would make me happy? Sammy moving back in with me."

"She's going to move back in by the end of next week no matter what, because that's when Laura and I are leaving. You were right, by the way, about spending more time with Sammy being good for our relationship. Being in the same building as the kids is not the same as living with them. I haven't been all that much better than the typical weekend dad, have I?"

"No, you haven't. I'm glad you've finally realized it. Parenthood isn't a hobby, Adam. It's a full-time job."

"Anyhow, they are pretty fantastic kids, Lizzie, both of them, and I give you most of the credit for that. Truce?"

"Truce. Now send me my daughter pronto, before I start liking you too much again."

SAMMY KNOCKED ON THE door a few minutes later. She did not have her knapsack, laptop, pillow, or any of her other belongings with her. But despite her disappointment, Liz swallowed hard, gave her daughter a kiss on the cheek and just asked, "How are you doing, Samwich?"

"You haven't called me that for years!"

"It just slipped out. I guess because I miss you so much. Do you realize that you've been living with your dad for a month already?"

"You have Josh. You have Jasper. You've got two big hairy guys to take care of you."

"I need my girl. What can I do to persuade you to come home?"

"Two things. Number one: give me more space. And number

two: stop treating me like I'm still a little kid. You let Josh come and go as he pleases and eat whatever he wants, and you never ask him who he's with or what time he's coming home, but you make a big fuss about every single thing I do even though you know I'm more responsible than he is!"

"That's not true, Sammy. Josh has the same curfew as you do and he's supposed to call and let me know where he is whenever he goes out. But anyway, I promise to let you have more independence."

"Good. So you should be glad to know that I'm getting my learner's permit next week. I've been studying the rules of the road with Daddy."

"I can't believe Adam would do something like that without consulting me." Feeling like her legs were about to buckle under her, Liz sat down heavily on the living room sofa.

"Why is this something you have to discuss with him?" Sammy spat angrily. "Everybody knows how to drive, Mum."

The reconciliation had been brief. So brief it felt like an illusion.

"Your brother doesn't," Liz offered, lamely.

"Actually, we're going to take Drivers' Ed together next term."

"Don't do it in the winter, Sammy, please! It gets dark so early, and the roads will be slippery and dangerous. Maxime and I nearly had a terrible accident when we went up north."

"That's exactly why we're going to take lessons in the winter. In case you haven't noticed, we live in Canada, where it's snowy half the year. Daddy thinks it's a good idea to get lessons during winter conditions."

"I see." Liz took a deep breath. The world insisted on moving on without her, taking her children into a future she feared.

But why did she fear it? Had she always?

"Mum? Are you okay?"

"Yes. I'm just feeling a little overwhelmed by everything that's happened recently, Sammy. Can I have a hug?"

"Only if you say that you approve of me learning to drive. I don't want to have another argument about this later."

"If that's the price of a hug, then yes, I approve of your learning how to drive. Your brother is another matter, however."

In spite of her indignation, Sammy had to laugh at that. She sat down on the sofa and gave her mother a hug.

"Anyhow, on the bright side, I suppose I should be happy you are friends with him again," Liz said.

"Josh is friends with Derek too. Don't look so surprised. I knew that would happen if they got to know each other. They like the same indie music, for one thing. You should hear them play together, it's really cool. Josh even invited Derek to join his band."

"I don't understand. Isn't Josh the lead guitarist?"

"Yes, but Derek is just as happy to play bass. And he sings way better than Josh does. They're planning to perform at the first school coffee house in the new year."

"Really?" Maybe this would be her chance to make amends. "Can I come? Are parents allowed to be in the audience?"

"Gee, I don't know, Mum, my school is pretty far away. You'd have to travel after the sun goes down, in the winter, with slippery sidewalks and dangerous people lurking in the shadows. Are you sure you'd feel safe?"

"Well, I'll have you there to protect me, Sammy. So I'll try to be brave."

A SMALL EVERGREEN TREE in the window of the shop filled the interior with the pungent smell of pine needles and a fire was burning in the hearth where Josh — who was supposed to be studying biology — sat thumbing through an out-of-date issue of the *Guinness Book of World Records*. He insisted that this counted as scientific research since the book was full of arcane data from every corner of the globe. Periodically he tried to entertain Liz and Georgia by reading them the strangest statistics he could find, mostly those having to do with repellent diseases and deformities, or fanatics dedicated to bizarre pursuits.

"Georgia, you've got to come see this guy; he's even got tattoos inside his mouth."

"'Most cockroaches ever eaten by a human being.' Hmm. How hungry would you have to be to try to beat that record?"

"Wow, this woman in Spain has a ninety-centimetre fingernail on her thumb. That's almost three feet. Hey, I've got a riddle for you guys. When is a fingernail not a fingernail? When it's three feet!"

The women just ignored him, concentrating instead on hanging dozens of yellow, red, and green dog biscuits from the tree with loops of red ribbon. Jasper prowled around happily behind them, snapping up all the broken and discarded pieces. But far from satisfying his appetite, these little snacks seemed merely to intensify it.

"Watch out, Mum, I think Jasper is scheming to eat your decorations right off the tree," Josh said. "He has a really devious look on his face. Like when Granny was here for Christmas two years ago and he stole all the leftover turkey from the sideboard."

"We'll have to put up some kind of barrier."

"What could keep Jasper away from food?" mused Georgia. "A vet armed with a needle?"

"No way," Liz laughed. "Jasper adores the vet. He tries to drag me in there every time we go past the office."

"Your dog is seriously disturbed, Mum."

"Well, maybe if you spent more time walking him you could mitigate my pernicious influence."

"Doesn't she know a lot of fancy words, Georgia?"

Into the middle of this lazy Sunday afternoon arrived Sammy and Derek.

"We were going to go skating at City Hall but it started snowing really hard so we gave up. Can we help you decorate the Dog instead?"

"Jasper looks just fine the way he is," Josh said. Once again, everyone ignored him.

"It's not fair. Nobody in this family ever laughs at my jokes," he whined.

"That's because jokes are supposed to be funny, Joshua, and yours are not," his sister explained, doing her most solemn impersonation of an elementary school teacher.

"I thought it was funny, Josh," Derek said. "It just took me a moment to figure out what you meant."

"Solidarity, dude," Josh replied solemnly, getting up from his undignified position and brushing off his knees. He and Derek then went through a complicated ritual of fist bumps, ending up back-to-back.

"That was way funnier than your joke, Josh," said his mother, smiling. It was hard for her to accept how quickly Derek had become part of the family, but she was trying her best to get over her mistrust of him. After all, she had done plenty of things she regretted in her own life, and other people had forgiven her.

"Derek, Sammy, if you two really want to help, I could use some inspiration for the mantelpiece. I don't want to hang up Christmas stockings. That's too predictable. Do you have any better ideas?"

"How about long johns?" suggested Georgia. "They would be much more appropriate for the weather."

"I have an idea," said Derek, tentatively. "Maybe we could pretend the wooden dogs on the mantel are Santa's reindeer. I saw a toy sleigh at the dollar store. We could string the dogs together with red ribbons or something and make them look like they were pulling it."

"That's brilliant, Derek," Sammy exclaimed. "Although all this heartwarming family togetherness makes it feels like we're in a really bad after-school special."

"Be as cynical as you like, young lady. I don't take times like these for granted anymore," said Liz.

As if on cue, Max walked in carrying a cake box.

"Oh lord," Sammy exclaimed. "See what I mean?"

"Beware of Classics professors bearing gifts," Georgia intoned ominously.

"Has anyone noticed that 'Beware of Greeks bearing gifts' is the opposite of 'Never look a gift horse in the mouth'?" Derek asked.

"A lot of proverbs contradict each other," Liz replied. "For example, I've often wondered why 'actions speak stronger than words' if the pen really is 'mightier than the sword.'"

"How about 'Two heads are better than one' and 'Too many cooks spoil the broth,' or 'Look before you leap' and 'He who hesitates is lost'?" Georgia suggested.

"Or 'Out of sight, out of mind' and 'Absence makes the heart grow fonder'?" offered Josh.

"You guys are completely nuts," Sammy said, giving in to laughter despite herself.

"Elizabeth, *ma belle*, why don't you go put the kettle on and I'll distribute this lovely cake," Max suggested, hanging his coat on the back of a chair.

Derek and Sammy curled up on the rug in front of the fire, Jasper quivering with anticipation beside them, ever vigilant for handouts. Josh returned to the sofa where Georgia and Max joined him, and a companionable silence descended on the room.

Liz came back a few minutes later, saying "It got so quiet in here I was worried," and then she almost dropped her tray full of mugs.

"Sammy, you're eating cake!"

"So?"

"So, I haven't seen you eating anything but carrot sticks, almonds, and clementines for a very long time."

"Well, Derek thinks I should eat more. He says that at work he's surrounded by girls who are constantly obsessing about their figures and they drive him nuts."

"I'd be more reassured if you had decided to be healthy on your own rather than doing it to please somebody else," Liz said, more acerbically than she had intended.

"First you're mad at me for *not* eating, and now you're mad at me for eating? I can't win with you, Mum, can I?" She threw her slice of cake in the wastebasket.

"That's not what she means, Sammy," Derek spoke, into the uncomfortable silence that followed.

Everyone looked at him.

"I'm sorry; I should just keep my big mouth shut," he said.

"No, Derek," Liz said. "I appreciate your support, really. Thank you. And Sammy, I'm sorry I was so stupid. Forgive me?"

"You have to back off, Mum. You promised."

"I know, I know. But it's easier said than done."

"Which reminds me of another expression I've never understood: 'easy as pie.' What's easy about pie, except eating it?" said Josh, gamely trying to deflect the tension.

"What about 'you can't have your cake and eat it too'?" Derek added. "That's even sillier."

Max was quick to recognize the diversion and continue it. "Surely what that means is that you can't have two mutually exclusive options. You have to choose one alternative or the other."

"Yeah, I get that, but it's a stupid illustration of the principle because, honestly, who would choose to keep their cake around instead of eating it?"

"Miss Havisham?" suggested Georgia.

"She's not a real person," Sammy objected. "It's cheating to support arguments about human nature with examples from literature."

"That's a controversial position to take, given that we're in a bookstore," Max observed. "Do you agree with your sister, Joshua?"

"Never. Which is why I think she needs more cake. Outside of a dog, cake is a girl's best friend."

"Inside of a dog, cake is pretty good too," said Liz, giving Jasper a fragment before scraping the rest of her piece onto Sammy's plate.

WHEN BRIAN finally showed up, all the time that had passed evaporated like spit on a griddle. It didn't matter that he had grown up and become responsible and that lots of people trusted him. It didn't matter that Natalie liked him; that he was going to tell her the whole story this weekend; that he'd finally dared to hope that she could hear the truth about him and still want to go out with him. It didn't matter that she was prepared to believe that he was a good person to whom terrible things had happened. Immediately he saw himself the way Brian did, as the white-faced little rat who had killed his mother.

And hadn't he always feared, deep in his fugitive soul, that Brian would find him someday? Why else had he changed his appearance and his name? No one besides Brian McKay would be looking for a blond guy named Andrew Scott. Not his own father, who had never looked back from the day he walked out the door, leaving nothing behind but his sperm donation and a couple of maxed-out credit cards. Not his pitiful mother or her sadistic boyfriend. Maybe it would have been better if her boyfriend had succeeded in killing him before Children's Aid took him away. Then he wouldn't have become an arsonist and a murderer. He wouldn't have had to endure years of nightmares: nightmares of Brian coming to get him, the prison-rapist coming to get him, the two merging together into a single old-young drunken lurching figure, throwing him to the ground hissing that he deserved what he was about to get.

And then laughing.

But now that Brian was here in the flesh he wasn't laughing. Older than the nightmare Brian, with a weathered face and thinning hair, he came into the nice Italian restaurant cursing that there was nowhere to park his fucking truck in this goddamn city. Seeing his foster brother after all this time so diminished, so angry, so lost, made him very glad that he'd refused to let the man meet him at the real estate office as he'd requested. How could he have explained their relationship to his colleagues? There was going to be a scene for sure, but at least here they could remain anonymous; just a couple of losers confronting each other in the big city.

Brian hardly ate a bite of his penne Calabrese. He looked around at the young men with pierced ears flirting with women in scanty clothing, at the flamboyantly bad art on the walls and ceiling, and was finally struck speechless when a slim-hipped waiter sauntered over with a giant wooden mill to ask if he'd like some pepper grated onto his food.

"Why the hell would I need extra pepper?" he replied. "Didn't you put enough in your sauce? At these prices, you'd better."

Seeing the restaurant through Brian's eyes made him embarrassed. He'd picked it because it was close to Forest Hill, where he'd been showing a couple of lawyers a three-million-dollar house, and because he remembered how much Brian had always loved spaghetti. He hadn't considered how pretentious the place might appear to someone from a small town in Northern Ontario.

Brian wasn't eating, though he was on his second beer. He tossed back his own glass of Sangiovese, pushed away his untouched plate of veal, took out his cellphone, checked his messages and said, "You know, I'm really not that hungry either. I need to go back to the office to do some paperwork. How long will you be in town for, Brian?"

"Don't give me the brush-off," said Brian. "We need to talk."

"I have to get up early tomorrow. This is the busy season for real estate. Everyone wants to sell their house once summer vacation is over and the kids are back at school but before the Christmas holidays."

"I don't give a damn about the real estate business. You owe me this, Scotty," Brian said.

He took a deep breath, putting his phone back in his pocket. "Okay. But I can't stay long."

"Isn't there somewhere we can go for a walk? This place is so fucking loud I can't hear myself think."

"It's raining, Brian. Besides which, I'm sure you're tired after that long drive. You want to get together tomorrow instead? I could take off a couple of hours in the early afternoon and show you around town."

"No, I do not want to get together tomorrow," Brian spat. "You know how long I've been waiting to talk to you? Seventeen fucking years."

"Okay, okay. Don't shout, Brian. You're upsetting other people."

"As if I care."

"Look, I just remembered. There's a kind of park a couple of blocks from here; will that do? We could walk around the pond."

"That's good," said Brian. "A pond is good. Do you still like to go fishing? We still get some pretty big muskie in the river back home."

"It's not that kind of pond. It's small, and nothing feeds into it anymore — the river's gone underground. The ducks and herons eat most of the fish before they get big."

"What use is a pond if you can't fish there?"

"Well, some people just like to look at it. It's pretty, you know."

"Just like you, Scotty. How'd you get so pretty?"

"I grew up, Brian. I changed. People change."

"No, they don't. That's a load of crap. You can dye your hair and wear expensive suits. You can carry a fucking briefcase and use a different name. But you'll always be the same devious little creep inside."

Embarrassed by the direction the conversation was taking, he signalled the waiter over and put their uneaten meals on his credit card, leaving a generous tip. He shrugged on his trench coat and left, avoiding the eyes of the other patrons. Brian followed, pulling out a pack of cigarettes from his ski-jacket pocket and lighting one the minute they were outside the restaurant. They drove in silence through the gate to Wychwood Park.

"Pull over to the right," he said, and winced as Brian plowed carelessly onto the verge of someone's garden, flattening a boxwood hedge.

It was darker there under the big trees, and cooler; he shivered, and turned up his collar. Brian lit another cigarette, delaying the conversation or working up to it. He would have felt better if they weren't the only people outside. Maybe the bad weather was keeping everyone indoors, or maybe it was just suppertime, or bath time, or story time — time for ordinary families to get on with their ordinary lives. Whatever the reason, nobody else saw fit to stroll around in the dark and wet.

All the houses they passed glowed with life; how he wished he were inside one of them! Instead, he led Brian down the hill towards the pond, stumbling a little in his thin-soled shoes. Brian was talking again: a long rambling monologue about how he'd been living up north with his father until the old man had a heart attack and died a few months ago. That's why he'd been looking for Scotty; in a weird kind of way, the bastard was the last family Brian had left. He even advertised in the paper back home to see if he wanted to come to the funeral, but of course, there was no reply.

But he couldn't give up. He had nothing to lose since he'd already lost everything. His mother, his home, and now his dad. And something else: his innocence. In the dark, under the trees, Brian confessed that he had always blamed himself for his mother's death, because he and Scotty both knew the fire was intended for him.

That he'd provoked it by tormenting Scotty, and therefore it was his fault.

Though he'd imagined this encounter a thousand times it had never occurred to him that Brian would feel guilty about what happened. He had no idea what to say, and was just starting to formulate a response — they were just kids then, kids do stupid things, it was time to forgive each other and go on with their lives — but Brian kept talking, spitting out the words like broken teeth from a mouth full of blood. Now he was saying that after his father died, he'd gone to the youth custody centre to find Scott. Somebody there said he went to Toronto to work in construction and gave him the phone number of another guy. And that guy was the one who told him he'd gone into real estate. Called him "Ghost," which, considering that it was Brian's mother that died, seemed kind of a bad joke.

There was no Andrew James Scott listed in the Toronto real estate business, but there was a plain old James Scott. So he took a chance and called the office, figuring it might be him because criminals always use aliases, don't they? So here he was. But he shouldn't have bothered. He should have known Scotty wouldn't care. Scotty never gave a shit about any of them.

He protested that he had always cared, and that he had never forgiven himself for the fire. That he was truly sorry to hear about Mr. McKay's death. But Brian just kept on interrupting him, not listening. Walking faster.

"You didn't just kill my mother. You killed my father too, because he never took care of his diabetes after she died. I had a good job in the Soo, but I had to leave it to move in with Dad after his first heart attack five years ago. He never remarried, you know. Or how would you know? Since you never even came back to see how we were."

Again he tried to say he was sorry and again Brian didn't hear him, ranting on now about the house, how they couldn't afford to rebuild it and besides, his father didn't have the energy. So they'd rented a shitty little bungalow closer to the mill. And that's where he'd gone to work when he left the Soo: the goddamn mill, not some fancy-ass real estate agency, because he had to take care of his dad, because his dad had nothing and nobody else. And now he had nothing either.

"But look what poor little neglected Andrew Scott has ended up with. A cushy job with all the perks. Life sure isn't fair."

Brian stopped by the tennis courts, out of breath with rage.

He tried to say, "I'm so sorry, I've always been sorry. I didn't mean to do it. Your mother was very good to me." He tried to say, "Can you ever forgive me?" But this time only a single strangled word, barely a whisper, came out: "Sorry." The rest of his appeal stuck fast in his throat and he felt like he was going to pass out, just as he did back then, when they told him what he'd done. Back when he realized that his single uncharacteristic act of defiance had killed somebody, somebody he liked, somebody who didn't deserve to die.

He stumbled away from Brian, grief-stricken, remorseful, trying to catch his breath. *Never turn your back on an enemy* was the rule he'd lived by in his old life. Too late, he realized that Brian was still his enemy and would never forgive him. Turning his elegantly clothed back on Brian was, in fact, the worst thing he could have done. It was also the last thing he did. He heard Brian curse, and felt unspeakable agony as something heavy crashed down on his head. What was it? He had no time to figure it out. He no longer had any time at all.

Acknowledgements

Thank you to Rachel Klein for helping me to get started, and to Gail Bowen for encouragement very early on when she was Writer in Residence at the Toronto Reference Library. Thanks also to others who read and made suggestions at various stages: Susan Free, Laurence Glickman, Lindsay Leonard, Carolyn Smart, and Chantal Tie Ten Quee. My gratitude to Detective Sergeant Peter Callahan of the Toronto police force for clarifying homicide procedure, Marlene Auspitz of Royal LePage for explaining real estate licensing, and Ann Buhay of the Toronto Reference Library for advice on how to track down old newspaper articles.

Extra treats to my dog Toby for walking tirelessly around Wychwood Park and for letting me rip off certain of his idiosyncrasies for my portrait of Jasper. Yes, Wychwood Park exists, ducks and all (though the fence has been moved from the edge of the water way up to the tennis court so the terrain no longer duplicates that in the story). I live near there in Hillcrest Village, which includes a lovely French patisserie specializing in gâteau basque. Like the bookstore, however, the characters and events depicted in this story are imaginary.

This is for all my friends in the 'hood.